HER DUKE AT DAYBREAK

MYTHIC DUKES
BOOK ONE

WENDY LACAPRA

Publisher:

Wendy LaCapra

http://www.wendylacapra.com/

Facebook * Twitter * Goodreads * Pinterest * Newsletter

Cover design by The Killion Group, Inc.

Developmental & Copy Editing by The Killion Group, Inc.

Ebook ISBN: 978–0-9994253–0-5

ISBN 10: 0–9994253–0-7

Print ISBN: 978–0-9994253–1-2

Manufactured in the United States of America

First Edition October 2017

❀ Created with Vellum

For Richard, Always

CHAPTER 1

*T*he Duke of Ashbey's mistress sent her goblet sailing past Ash's cheek, lifting a lock of his hair. The fine flint glass shattered against the wall behind him.

Alas. The servants were going to have a devil of a time picking the shards out of the carpet.

"My dear, is that any way to treat a gift?"

The delicate features of Miss Eliza White—Madame Elisabetta Bianci to her legion of admirers—splotched. "Name the occasion upon which you presented them to me, and I will spare the rest."

Ash hadn't the faintest. Although if he properly recalled, his secretary had traveled all the way to Waterford for those glasses. *Pity.* He steepled his fingers and tapped them against his lips.

Had he gifted them to her on her birthday? Unlikely. He'd never asked the exact date of her birth. Anniversary? Doubtful as well. Their first coupling had taken place on an indeterminate evening sometime around Michaelmas…or had it been the feast of St. Stephen?

The air had been cold, anyway.

He snapped his fingers. "The night you opened in The Tempest." *Ah, well.* A glass soared over his head. Now they were down to three. "Liza, must you punctuate with Penrose glass?" Only two remained. He rubbed his forehead. "Despite what you may believe, I would hate to see you hurt."

"Hurt?" She lifted the penultimate goblet in a bitter mock toast. "How dare you speak to me of hurt?" She emphasized *you* with repugnance appropriate to rotting excrement.

Undeserved repugnance, really. He'd been referring to injured flesh, not injured sentiment.

Gently, very gently, he posed a question. "Have I ever lied to you?"

The goblet careened past his ear. Five glasses had not improved her aim, thank goodness.

"You lie by existing." Her chest heaved. "A man without feeling is no man at all."

Many might agree. Regrettably, he could not provide the satisfaction of a reaction.

Poor Liza.

His gaze caressed her figure.

She deserved offerings more particular to her person than carnal indulgence. She'd been obliging, and until tonight, seemingly unconcerned with his lack of sentiment.

"Can you think of nothing to say?" She blinked, goblet aloft.

She had such pretty eyes, with sickle-curved lashes black as coal. When she'd been introduced to Ash, her eyes had been windows to an exuberant soul. Now they glowed like Hades, the delight within them having vanished.

"Nothing at all?!" Her voice rose to a fevered pitch. She fisted her goblet-free hand against her hip.

Rather, the vicinity of her hip.

Tightly laced stays may have enhanced her bosom, but they ruined her intended effect.

"You are the one ending our arrangement," he pointed out,

ever aware of the final glass. "Can you blame me for assuming you were not interested in my say?"

She gasped. "For eighteen months—"

That long?

"—you have been coddled—"

True.

"—diverted—"

Somewhat.

"—*satisfied*."

Unfortunately, not. Saying so, however, would have been unforgivably rude. He was incapable of feeling—that much was indisputable. But Heaven forbid he forgo manners. A man had to have some standards.

"You performed your duties to perfection," he conceded.

A feline sound emanated from her lips. "Everyone warned me—"

"Myself included."

"—your murderous, cold-blooded heritage would manifest."

How trite of her to resort to the obvious.

"My father was *tried* for murder, not convicted." He paused. "Clarity is important."

"You—" she pointed at his chest as if he were the one on trial "—are as mad as they say he was."

"Doubtful. Again, clarity. My father kept crickets as pets." He rubbed his chin and then leaned back in his chair. "And, he may, or may not, have skewered his valet and deposited the body atop his wife."

Ash's father had not been convicted because the only witness, Ash's mother, had fled the country that day. The court had only his father's description. And his father, as everyone knew, had been—from childhood—mad as a Bedlam scrub.

"How can you speak of horrors in such a flippant tone?" She paled. "Is nothing inviolate to you?"

Interesting question. "I cannot think of an exception."

Her huff blew a loosened curl from her face. "Honestly, I begin to understand why your wife preferred death to—"

Later, he would not remember leaping from the chair. Nor extending his hand toward Liza. Now, however, he was, and would remain, infinitely relieved he stopped short of wrapping his fingers around his former lover's throat.

He dropped his arm and stepped back. Deliberately, he interlocked his hands behind his back.

"Miss White." His enunciated syllables were whisper-soft. "You have freely taken everything I promised. And you have stated your wish to end our liaison." He leveled his gaze. "Now I will wish you well, and you will promise to vacate this house by quarter's end."

She slammed her fist against the table. The glass in her hand fractured into slivers. Her face twisted in shock and pain, and blood seeped from the open wound.

"Look!" she screeched. "Look what you've done!"

Calmly he lifted her arm, and with his free hand, he rang the bell. This was exactly the sort of thing he'd been trying to prevent.

"Unhand me." She tore herself away.

Probably best. A maid appeared at the door. Her eyes widened, and she rushed toward her mistress.

"Careful!"

He reached out to guide the maid around the broken glass, but she skittered beyond his reach, more frightened of him than the glass.

"Get out." Liza's voice was filled with loathing. The maid drew back. "Him—not you." Liza allowed herself to be tended without moving her gaze. "You have taken much from me, Duke. But nothing I cannot recover. And do you know why?"

Rhetorical, of course. Obligingly, he waited for the linguistic slap.

"Because *I* have a heart."

"That you do," he acknowledged with a bow.

He instructed the maid to send for a doctor before turning toward the hall. Eighteen months had been too long an association. A mistake he would not make again. He hadn't the will nor the wish to ruin anymore lives.

No matter how clear the terms, the longer one danced with a devil the more destructive the burn.

"Ashbey?" Liza called.

He looked over his shoulder.

"May you rot in the darkness you have chosen."

With that, his once-vibrant mistress crumbled into a heap on the floor, her lace cuffs stained with blood. Ash continued through the door. At least *she* was alive. Not so, the woman he married.

Rachel had, in fact, preferred death to a lifetime with him.

His mind filled with a haze of smoke and the hideous sound of ancient rafters breaking free. The bodies of his wife and his father had been discovered in the wreckage of Wisterley's north wing. His father's, still locked in the rooms where he'd been, for a decade, confined. And his wife, just a few feet away from escaping the blaze she'd purposely set.

Ash had tried to forcibly remove her, and he doubted she'd wrested free of his grasp to save the duke. She'd barred others from reaching his father's door with the declaration he deserved to die.

Which left only one explanation—she could not endure one more day as his wife.

A cold shiver passed through his veins. Then, the townhouse door clicked closed—bringing him back, and marking the end of another life chapter.

He continued onward, but night's soothing darkness did little to mellow his mood. The path to his home journeyed through streets far from London's worst, yet there was still some chance he'd meet a cutthroat. Honestly, he'd welcome physical pain.

He strove to shield others from his inner maelstrom, but, tonight, the curses of those he'd unintentionally damned had become incessant crickets, chirping in the twisted thicket of his soul. The most recent curse, however, had been wrong on one, important point. He'd never *chosen* the darkness.

The darkness had chosen him.

"IMPOSSIBLE!" Aunt Hester spoke in a tone that brokered no objection.

The little man from the Admiralty—the one with the sheets of vellum and the satchel—bounced his knee. A subtle bounce, but a bounce nonetheless. Alicia noticed, because no one else in the room moved.

Not Aunt Hester—Alicia's recently deceased husband's aunt. Aunt Hester's face had frozen in mutinous disbelief.

Not the captain—his guilt-stricken eyes and absent limb remained still.

And certainly not Alicia herself—sitting stiff-backed and without visible expression. She was annoyed, however. The little man's twitch was disturbing their tableau.

Gentlemen Deliver Distressing News.

They had not created a perfect tableau. A more visual depiction of woe would have been *de rigueur*. But since she had been forced to conceal her response to the thousand daily humiliations inflicted on a publicly spurned wife, Alicia's reaction was bound to lack potency.

Perhaps she could improve the scene if she bent her body with grief, lifting tear-stricken eyes to the heavens...

The celebrated painter Romney had captured the countess in

just such a pose. But surely, the countess would not quibble if Alicia stole the posture, not when the countess had stolen Alicia's husband, keeping him enthralled until his death. And now, according to these men, there was a good chance the countess could take full possession of the Stone estate and its income.

"We are pursuing the validity of the death-bed codicil to the admiral's will," the little man assured.

"Tell them." Aunt Hester's chest pulsed with shallow breath. "Tell them the admiral would never have made such an outrageous arrangement. Astonbury has been in the family for decades."

Untrue. Octavius had purchased Astonbury with war spoils less than ten years past. It only *seemed* longer. She and Aunt Hester and Octavius's brother Simon hadn't lived there for an age. Not since Octavius moved the countess and their child into the home.

"Lady Stone," Aunt Hester snapped.

Lady. She'd never grown used to being addressed as such. Then again, by the time Octavius became a viscount, she'd been effectively sliced from his life.

"Alicia." Hester's sigh was wracked with aggravation. "I asked you to speak."

Speak. Yes, of course. But what should she say? Alicia's eyes settled on the captain.

His sun-soaked skin had the leathery texture that made most sailors look hard, but there was something compelling about him. She searched his strange, haunted gaze. His features were tempered with forbearance present only in those whom great hardship had touched.

"You seem very familiar, Captain," Alicia said. "Have we met?"

The little man's head snapped toward the captain, but the captain's features softened. "I was a young officer on *The Maitland*."

Ah. Octavius's first ship. She forced her mind back, searching. No memory of an officer named Smith surfaced. Instead, the sensation of heat rushed over her skin, followed by the echoing sound of water. Azure water, so clear you could spot a fish from the bow of a frigate. And Octavius. Sparkling brighter than the sun on the waves. Her hero.

England's hero.

And the countess's fallen lover.

"Octavius is gone." For her, he'd been gone for a very long time.

"Yes," the captain answered—communicating so much more than a single syllable should—the weight of soured hopes and youthful follies, of plans gone awry and consequent dismay. And grief. An ocean full of grief.

"Is she well?" The little man's question dried the mist in Alicia's eyes.

Aunt Hester *tsked*. "How did you expect her to react? She's just learned we've been left destitute, and her husband's mistress will receive everything."

The captain answered, "The Admiralty will, of course, take the admiral's family into consideration."

Odd that, when Octavius had not.

Then again, he *had* taken his family into consideration, hadn't he? In the codicil, he'd claimed the countess and her illegitimate daughter, who had been his by every right but law. Now they would have everything that was his, too.

One had to admit a kind of justice, however painful.

"The Admiralty," Hester argued, "has not the means nor the will to provide for a fallen sailor."

"Your nephew was hardly just a sailor," the little man cut in. "He died whilst winning a brilliant battle. A posthumous elevation is being discussed."

Alicia bit back an unladylike snort. Was she to become not just a lady, but a countess? On equal footing as her rival.

Except childless.

Without Octavius's estate or its income and with Octavius's younger brother—currently at sea—and his spinster aunt in her care.

"The codicil will not stand," Aunt Hester said. "We will go to the courts."

The captain cleared his throat. "Courts will not be necessary. The Admiralty has asked me to assist in finding a resolution."

So that explained the captain's presence—he had been tasked with tidying up. The Admiralty wanted to smooth Octavius's messy wake so their hero could shine in death.

"We are attempting to reach Simon's ship," the Captain continued.

"Simon?" Alicia frowned. What had Octavius's brother to do with this?

"He must come home, of course," the little man said.

Simon was going to be furious if forced to leave the Navy. She must write to reassure—*Oh.*

Everything became clear.

The Admiralty needed a male. For the title, of course. And they needed a title to distract the public.

Even though the title had been bestowed on Octavius by valor and not by birthright, they would transfer it to Simon and then push him to the front of the nation's imagination with pomp and circumstance and an immaculately powdered wig. And in turn, *the heir* would push the grieving gaggle of women forever bound together by scandal into the background where, no doubt, the Admiralty believed they belonged.

The Admiralty expected her to silently wait for them to resolve her financial difficulties while they crafted the narrative.

Waiting, she understood. One could go mad from waiting. Airless, ravenous waiting in a cold and lifeless bed. She boxed the shame and humiliation and anger and slid them securely into the shadows.

The minutiae of living would not cease while the Admiralty executed their plan. Melodrama did not interrupt the need for shelter and for food. The quarterly bills would be due in a fortnight. And Cook had said something about the store of flour, had she not?

The future yawned in a dizzying expanse.

Concentrate, Alicia. Details, not sentiments.

The income from her marriage settlement would keep them for a time, but not in their current mode of living. And not with Octavius's debts.

She looked around the sitting room. This house could be let. They could retire to smaller lodgings in some place less fashionable than London. Bath, perhaps? The surrounding countryside would be good for her soul. Aunt Hester would appreciate taking the waters.

Alicia's gaze slid to Aunt Hester's pinched mouth.

Or not.

What mattered was they would get by, no matter what these men decided was best.

They would economize. Something that would—ironically—be easier without Octavius's expensive tastes. Life would be less luxurious, of course. But they would have enough to eat. And they would have each other.

"If you'll excuse us, Captain." She stood. As expected, every person in the room followed her lead.

"Of course," the captain replied. "We have taken too much of your time already."

"Not at all." She allowed him to take her hand. "We appreciate the courtesy."

"We will be in touch." He gave her another deep look of understanding.

Too deep.

Her feelings were not for consumption. Especially not by the

Admiralty, who were determined to package up Octavius's loved ones in shackles topped with a pretty, iron bow.

She smiled sweetly as the captain and the little man departed.

The Admiralty may be determined. But she was equally determined she would never don shackles again.

CHAPTER 2

*a*sh sat alone within his study, the only inhabited room in his London home save the kitchens. He ate, drank, worked, read, and slept within these walls—his cocoon in a cavernous house stuffed full of macabre memories. Earlier, he'd declined to have his manservant, Kent, light the lamps. Tonight, he preferred shadow.

He always preferred shadow, truth be told.

May you rot in the darkness you have chosen...

He scowled. What the devil was wrong with darkness, anyway? Why this universal mania for light? He'd always been intrigued by the description of what came *before* the sun's creation.

Now the earth was formless and empty, darkness was over the surface of the deep...

Ah, he loved the sound of the deep. *The deep* was a place one could rest.

Formless, like broken crystal.

Empty, like the chambers of his heart. He rubbed his fingers against his chest.

Although plenty of evidence had mounted to the contrary, he did possess a functional version of the organ. Somewhere beneath his ribs, his heart swished like a sponge in seawater on a moonless night. The organ's stubborn persistence was the only reason he remained afloat on the surface of the dark deep.

Alive, yes. But for what purpose?

He'd long suspected Purpose, with a capital P, did not exist.

And yet there was something, wasn't there? A sense there was more. A sense kindled by having born witness to another's love. A love that had been transformative, mysterious and grand.

Such an experience was not for him. Never for him. His home —his life—had always been engulfed by gloom. He had survived, but the gloom had taken his father's reason, his mother's maternal responsibility, and his wife's life.

Yet, sometimes...*sometimes*...he could almost believe his life was being held in abeyance, as if he were a shade of the dead, and could be reanimated with the proper sacrifice. In those times, hope, in wraith form, flitted at the edge of his senses, a blessing and a curse.

Ash squeezed his eyes closed, gathering silence into his mind. Silence dulled thoughts' sharp edges, lulling him to stillness, a vacant sort of peace.

Time passed while he remained suspended—an hour? Maybe more—until a commotion sounded outside his door.

"...in the study, I'll wager."

Hurtheven. He snorted. The man always appeared when least desired.

May you rot in the darkness you have chosen...

Right. Well, perhaps he could use a visit, desired or not.

"Your Grace." Kent spoke to the Duke of Hurtheven with awe the manservant never quite mustered for Ash. Then again, he'd been the only servant who'd refused to settle elsewhere after the fire. "His Grace is not receiving."

"Excellent," Hurtheven replied. "Then we shall not be disturbed. And Kent?"

"Yes, Your Grace?"

"Ash never receives."

"Quite so, Your Grace."

The door flew open.

"Christ! A bat could not find his way in here."

Struck by another voice, a voice he hadn't heard in six long years, Ash stood so fast, he knocked over his chair.

"Chev!?" Ash gazed at his old ally in disbelief. Even Cheverley's wife, though loyal, was said to have given up hope the man was alive.

Hurtheven shushed. "Cheverley remains among the missing," he said, giving a pointed look to the back of the servant still in the room. "Allow me to introduce Captain Smith, future occupant—we hope—of your uninhabited upper rooms. Captain Smith is the Admiralty's man in charge of—" His sentence ended abruptly.

Kent lit the last sconce and then slipped from the room.

"What is it you are doing for the Admiralty, Smith?" Hurtheven asked.

"Nefarious deeds." Chev stepped out from behind Hurtheven with a bitter exhale.

Ash's long-absent companion, one-third of a secret society that dated back to their Eton days, had returned absent the lower portion of his arm.

His *right* arm.

"The Admiralty," Chev said, "feels I can be of more use on land."

Damnation! At least he was alive. "I do not understand." Ash frowned. After six interminable years, Ash expected Cheverley to be anxious to see his once-beloved wife. "Why must you stay here? Does Pen know you have returned?"

Hurtheven answered. "The Admiralty knows, I know. And now you know."

Chev's gaze remained blank. "Hurtheven said your staff consists of a manservant and his wife."

"A discreet manservant," Hurtheven added. "Since Chev must remain missing"—Hurtheven exchanged a meaningful glance with Cheverley—"for now, I thought your rooms could provide comfort and concealment."

Ash remembered to shut his mouth. "Concealment, yes." His home had never provided comfort. "You may stay, of course."

He preferred solitude. So much so he'd closed every room in the house. But this was Cheverley. Chev and Hurtheven remained his oldest, and only, allies. No one survived boarding school without allies, not even the son of a mad, murderous duke.

Or especially the son of a mad, murderous duke, as the unsubtle Hurtheven told the tale.

"If you become a restive host"—Hurtheven smiled—"you can always seek comfort in Bianci's arms."

San subtlety point proven.

"Unfortunately," Ash said, "the St. John's Wood house will soon be vacant."

"Finally thrown over, were you?" Hurtheven asked.

"Yes." Finally?

"I am astonished she lasted, truth be told. Are you feeling—"

Ash raised his brows.

"Of course not." Hurtheven clapped him on the shoulder. "I am parched, many thanks for asking. And Smith here would welcome a seat, I am sure."

"Yes, of course." Ash shook his head to clear the obvious haze. It wasn't every night he found himself unceremoniously discarded by his mistress only to discover a long-dead friend very much alive. Alive...but hiding. "Please, take a seat."

Ash retrieved scotch from his cabinet and poured three

fingers. He handed the first to Hurtheven and the second to Chev.

The years had been less than kind to Cheverley, though the determined set of his friend's chin remained familiar. As did that quality Cheverley possessed when he fixed Ash with his disturbing pale gaze—the one that made Ash feel his secrets were as obvious as his cravat.

"Heartily glad to have you here," Ash said.

Chev nodded his thanks. Ash looked away from Chev's tremor. Some things a man did not wish acknowledged, even by an old ally.

"So," Hurtheven turned to Cheverley, "six years is a long time to cover. Where shall I begin?"

"Why don't you abridge?" Chev suggested.

"Ashbey," Hurtheven gestured toward Ash, "has been doing the utmost to fulfill his Eta Rho Zeta sobriquet."

"Eta Rho Zeta." Chev's lip nearly lifted into a smile. The levity passed. "I haven't heard that silly name in an eternity."

"A secret society should always have a name," Hurtheven replied. "Does it matter if we borrowed whimsy from the colonies when choosing ours?" Hurtheven toasted the sky. "With appreciation to my uncle, the traitorous Virginian."

"I believe," Ash said, "they call themselves Americans."

"Never mind the usurpers." Hurtheven drank again. "Let a meeting of the Olympians commence. "Hades." He nodded to Ash. "Poseidon." His gaze moved to Chev. "And"—he toasted himself—"Zeus."

"Aren't we a little old for this?" Ash asked.

"Gods live forever," Hurtheven answered.

Cheverley made a dismissive sound. "Someone should have informed the French."

"You returned, did you not?" Hurtheven pointed out.

No subtlety at all.

Ash cleared his throat. "Che—Smith, I mean—how long do

you expect to stay in London?"

"I am not sure." Cheverley swirled the liquid in his glass. The circles under his eyes appeared to darken. "I've been tasked with a sordid affair."

"Why not place it before the council?" Hurtheven asked. "As always, you may depend on our discretion."

"You aren't even here, are you?" Ash added.

"Right," Chev answered with a curt nod. "The mess concerns Admiral Octavius Stone—"

"Recently deceased hero of the hour?" Hurtheven interrupted.

Chev cut him a look and started again. "Admiral Stone's doctor has produced a codicil to his will, dictated, supposedly, on his death bed."

"The report said he died in battle."

"Actually, no. He died later."

"Rather spoils the story of the dramatic death on deck."

Chev grimaced. "It happened just as described, except he lingered for a gruesomely painful hour. Enough time to dictate a codicil to his will, leaving his legitimate family penniless and his mistress enriched."

"Allow me to guess." Hurtheven's tone dripped with sarcasm. "The Admiralty, out of altruistic kindness, is concerned for the widow."

Chev rubbed his head. "They are concerned, as you well know, with the public. Stone went so far as to request his bastard daughter be given his name."

Gossip was one level of hell Ash avoided, but even *he* had heard of Admiral Stone and his love affair with an exceptionally alluring actress-turned-countess and one-time muse of the nation's most celebrated portrait artist. By all reports, the admiral had been devoted to his mistress and their child.

"From a distance," Ash said, "what the Admiralty deems an embarrassment appears to be quite just."

"His wife would be penniless but for what she brought to the marriage. His *wife*, Ash." Chev's voice vibrated with uncharacteristic anger. "The woman he swore to honor and protect."

Ash caught Hurtheven's eye, and heard Hurtheven's thoughts as if he had spoken them aloud. *Cheverley should be less concerned with the admiral's wife and more concerned with his own.*

When they'd been young and foolish, Ash and Hurtheven had helped Cheverley elope—a dramatic affair involving a stolen carriage hurtling over dark roads toward Scotland. But the elopement had happened a lifetime ago. Ash's gaze traveled back to Cheverley. Neither he nor Hurtheven knew what Chev had experienced these past six years.

Ash expected Chev had a reason for not rushing home, and it was not his place to inquire.

"I've been to visit Lady Stone," Chev said.

"Is she as frigid and cold as everyone says?" Hurtheven sounded hopeful.

Chev glanced up, startled. "I would not call her cold, though she's grown more reserved over the years."

"You know her then?" Ash asked.

"Does that not compromise your identity?" Hurtheven added.

"I did not think she would remember me. And she did not." Chev rubbed his forehead. "Not by name, anyway. She asked if we met. I told her I was a young officer on Stone's ship."

"Were you?" Ash asked.

Chev nodded. "My first Atlantic crossing happened to be the fateful voyage that brought Stone to meet his wife. Stone cast himself as the hero in a dramatic rescue, and they wed in haste."

"Much like yourself," Hurtheven murmured.

Chev's annoyed glance melted as he nodded in acknowledgment of the truth.

"I had forgotten," Cheverley's voice grew distant.

"Forgotten what?" Ash asked.

"I'd forgotten how taken I'd been by Lady Stone. She possesses an otherworldly quality—an expressive, almost angelic, face. Had I not been wed, even I would have been tempted to offer my protection."

Ash blinked, leaning forward as if catching a scent. He had never heard that tone from Chev. Not for anyone else but Pen.

"Just the opposite of the countess," Hurtheven observed, "who is so eager to please, every word she utters is excitement-infused and drips with invitation."

"Lady Stone has an altogether different kind of allure," Chev said. "A guileless grace, as if she could make a broken man whole just by standing by his side." Chev sighed. "It's damn seductive—unintentionally so. We were all half in love."

A broken man made whole. Ash could hardly imagine receiving such a woman's favor. If Chev, whose wife gazed at him in adoration, had been so affected, what must this woman be like?

Something covetous slid, serpent-like, through the recesses of Ash's mind. Hope's wraith danced past his gaze. A feminine silhouette. A sweet sigh. Delicious, trusting softness. Proffered lips, tasting of Lethe's elixir.

"I'd like to meet her." Ash's declaration surprised him as much as anyone else.

Chev glanced up sharply.

"You?" Hurtheven asked.

Ash arched a brow. "Is it so odd?"

"Well," Hurtheven paused, "yes. Geniality is not generally part of your character."

Ash could hardly argue there.

Chev set down his drink. "The answer is no."

"No?" No was not a word Ash heard often.

In this case, it shoved him in the chest, thrusting him back in his place—the unwilling, lonely lord of the underworld. But the covetous reptile hissed, lifting its head and turning its yellowed crescent eyes toward the phantom image of Lady Stone.

"She's not for you." Chev's sigh softened his tone. "Lady Stone is embroiled in scandal enough as it is."

Ash looked away. "Of course, she is not for me." He was Hades. Hell was his home. He shrugged. "Far be it from me to taint her angelic wings."

But the serpent's fangs dripped with venom just the same. Venom strong enough to subdue any prey.

CHAPTER 3

*T*he air was crisp and cold the morning Admiral Octavius Stone was finally laid to rest.

The Admiralty had lauded their fallen hero with an immaculately planned, multi-day affair. As for Alicia, the countess, and their respective households, they had been advised to remain in their homes, behind closed and bolted doors.

In the evenings, Aunt Hester read the reports.

The *Times* implored the citizens of London to cease marching wax effigies of the admiral through the streets, as such displays were unbecoming to the courage and dignity of the deceased.

The *Herald* favorably reviewed the battle reenactments played to sold-out audiences in Drury Lane.

And other papers—the kind Alicia only dared to read after Aunt Hester retired—described how the distraught countess received visitors from her bed while clutching the now blood-stained coat Octavius had been wearing when a musket ball ripped through his shoulder and lodged in his spine.

Alicia spent an inordinate amount of time thinking about that musket ball.

It seemed absurd that after all Octavius's daring, all his courage, and all his strength, one tiny lead ball could demand such a larger-than-life figure pay the ultimate price.

Thinking of that musket ball left tears in Alicia's eyes; remembering her husband did not.

The musket ball had destroyed a once-in-a-century strategist born with the sole purpose of saving the seas. The husband she remembered destroyed her heart. In defense of the towering figure felled by the musket ball, the Admiralty acted to conceal Octavius's past. Because of the humiliation she'd suffered at the hands of the often selfish, ever inconsiderate Octavius, Alicia complied.

So, while fifteen thousand viewed Octavius in state, Alicia stitched closed holes in Aunt Hester's hose. While ten times that number crowded boat decks and clung to rigging waiting for a glimpse of the admiral's funeral barge, she soothed Aunt Hester's spirits, reading from the Book of Psalms.

By the day of the land procession to the tomb in St. Paul's, Alicia believed she had successfully prevented the mourning mania gripping London from breeching her household's defense. But truth, thick as wood smoke, had seeped under the latch, scuttled across the floors and burrowed into the creases of Aunt Hester's brow.

"Every inhabitant in England will be lining the streets," Hester huffed. "Surely his own family has a right to be there."

Alicia looked up from her sewing. Aunt Hester usually insisted on propriety, however, her nerves were frequently rattled, and she was often unable to comprehend events in any other way but the way she was affected.

"Ladies of rank rarely attend funerals," Alicia reminded.

"I do not wish to attend the funeral," Hester gritted. "I wish to see the procession."

"We cannot." Alicia's tone sent a clear, full stop. "Do not be fooled. These throngs of people see your nephew's death as little more than an exciting distraction." Even she knew she lied.

Hester began to pace. "We are to be draped in black, then." She sniffed. "Condemned to mourn in silence while the whole world *wails*."

Not, unfortunately, an exaggeration. For the past few days, collective sobbing had become an accompaniment to London's already cacophonous song. While they had lost, respectively, a neglectful nephew and adulterous husband, the rest of the world had lost the vanquisher of Napoleon's ships, the savior of the nation, and one half of a legendary love affair.

"We must remain here because of *her*," Hester said with acid. "*Her* and her bastard child."

In her mind's eye, Alicia saw a weeping woman and child huddled together in a bed, wrapped in a bloodied coat. Like a reprimand from beyond, a cold sensation lifted the hair on her neck. She set aside her book.

"The countess grieves as we grieve."

Hester's eyes narrowed. "Are you grieving, Alicia? *Are you?*"

The accusing question hit Alicia like a physical blow.

"Very well, we will go. But you must promise me you will remain silent. If we are seen, you know what kind of sensation that would cause."

Before she thought through a plan, she was guiding a heavily veiled Hester down the front stairs and along the city streets. A task her own heavy veil made difficult.

By the time the two reached the route, the crowd had grown several layers thick. To Alicia's amazement, an accommodating group of Gentlemen parted one by one, helping Alicia and Hester to the front.

Standing shoulder to shoulder with strangers, all in a state of strange, anticipatory anguish, added flourish to the already unreadable script in her heart. Then, a murmur swelled in the crowds.

The chief mourners passed—members of the Admiralty, she suspected. If she'd been Octavius's wife in truth, she would have known them by name.

She did not. And her shame was complete. Patriotism, however, formed an efficient cloak. As a British subject, she could stand in gratitude for Octavius's service and mourn his sacrifice.

A stubborn clog of God-knew-what caught in her throat as the velvet canopy came into view. The canopy covered the admiral's mahogany casket, adorned with scenes of his heroism.

How was it possible Octavius lay within? How was any of this possible? By all rights she should be back on her island. She did not belong here.

She did not belong anywhere.

Aunt Hester's hand squeezed hers. The neglectful nephew was still a nephew. The absent husband was still the man Alicia had sworn to love.

"Let's go," Aunt Hester choked as she spoke.

Like a beast waking from slumber, the crowd began to move. Alicia wrapped one arm firmly through her Aunt's, but her veil muffled every "Pardon" and "Please make way."

"Please—please get us out." Aunt Hester's quivering voice sounded close to Alicia's ear.

She could not see, confound her foolish decision to come out into this mess. With a sweep of her hand, she lifted her veil. Using her firmest voice, she demanded a path. Slowly they made their way through the mass of humanity surging toward St. Paul's. She maneuvered them to the shelter of a vendor's cart and stood at Aunt Hester's side, rubbing her back as she silently wept.

"Aw."

Alicia glanced around, catching the eye of an elderly female vendor.

"Broken up over the loss of the handsome gent, is she?" the vendor asked.

The vendor must have mistaken Aunt Hester's petite form for that of a child. Alicia dared not contradict. She nodded.

"We *all* are." A young woman looked up from browsing funeral mementos, clearly affronted by the suggestion anyone could experience grief for the fallen hero equal to her own. "Imagine what his *family* feels." She selected a print from the vendor and sighed. "So, so sad."

Alicia had seen the likeness of Octavius often enough to blunt its effect. However, in this version, the weeping angel on his left looked a great deal like the countess. And the kneeling child on his right, Octavia.

The vendor dabbed her eyes—eyes undoubtedly fixed on a sale. "Touches the heart, it does." She pointed to the child in prayer. "His daughter," she whispered. "Very accomplished, they say."

"Of course, she is. She was born of beauty and bravery." The woman sighed again, deeper this time, as she handed over a coin. "The countess would have made the admiral the perfect wife if the barren shrew he married had the grace to die."

The pain Alicia had released impacted her chest in dizzying rebound. Aunt Hester slipped an arm through hers and tugged, but she remained rooted. Fixed to the very spot as every emotion she'd suppressed suddenly ran riot through her mind.

Rage.

Devastation.

Pain.

Pain, as unforgiving and inescapable as a humid high noon in her tropic home.

And then another type of burn, as if she were being watched. She turned, instantly locking gazes with a man. His black hair teased his collar with a hint of wave. His symmetric nose complemented his unforgettably firm mouth. He was alive and vivid, pulsing with an arresting consciousness at odds with the mourning throngs.

Something in her chest cleaved.

He *saw*. He saw the heartlessness of the woman's statements. He saw the truth of them, as well. In short, he saw Alicia's most closely guarded secret—the aching loneliness at the center of her heart.

Somehow, she'd unwittingly shared a more honest part of her than she'd ever shared. Alicia had been cast off, shut out. She'd wanted desperately to be let back in, yet had known the struggle was futile—the door had forever closed.

Worse still, this truth was reflected in the handsome stranger's eyes. His sympathetic expression left her wanting dreadfully to be held.

ASH'S GAZE fixed on the widow and a lightning bolt hit his chest.

She was no longer veiled as she'd been when he'd followed her from her home—the effect was glorious dawn. Not strictly a youth, she was neither a matron. Her light hair curled in discordant wisps around a soft face so lovely and luminous he nearly doubled over.

She was everything Chev had described and more. And she was standing just beyond his reach.

He'd refused to look away when her gaze met his, though his behavior was rude. He'd refused to look away because her gaze, full of tortured emotion, clashed with her presence.

Tortured emotion, he understood.

A sensation, long frozen, burst free from his chest—pain. Pain, and grief-stricken anger, both suspended in yawning loneliness. The emotions—Good God—they cut through him with the messy imprecision of a surgeon's saw.

He was feeling. Not just observing, but *feeling*.

They had not even met, and Lady Stone had accomplished the impossible—she had made him feel.

In the weeks following Cheverley's warning, he'd poured through his library archives, striving to find any mention of her name.

Early papers described the then-captain's young bride in praise-worthy, though suspicious terms—she'd not been born on British soil, after all. She was not, therefore, one of them. Then Admiral Stone met the countess, who fell into his arms in grateful tears after his victorious fleet arrived in Sicily where she'd been stranded by war.

The countess was already a legend—a vivacious siren with a titillating past. Beauty had indeed met bravery. England collectively swooned. Lady Stone was cast out as the unwanted specter marring a world belonging to undeniably genuine—if salacious—love.

Ash understood the wilderness beyond society's castle walls. He understood the lonely longing to be let back inside. And so he'd become even more determined they meet.

In Ash's dark dreams, she became a cinder pathway beneath his feet. In his noonday reflections, she became his muse.

His absorption wasn't rational.

It was not even sane.

Yet his dreams persisted.

Covet was too pithy a word for a force capable of thieving a man's reason.

And now that he had seen her pain, he wanted to take her away. Away from the hordes jockeying for a glimpse of the admiral's casket. Away from these women and their words, sharp as pointed shards. But away to where? *Wisterley*, half in ruin?

She's embroiled in scandal enough as it is.

"Blind me!" The vendor stared at Lady Stone. "Aren't you the admiral's—?"

"No," Ash answered sharply. "My wife resembles her, yes. But I am sorry to disappoint. My dear, shall we return to the carriage? I fear the crowds have grown too thick for Felicia."

Stupid to have chosen a name so close to her own. Too late, however, to amend.

He extended his arm to Lady Stone. She hesitated only a moment.

"Yes," she replied.

She dropped her veil, and leaned down to whisper something in her companion's ear. The companion nodded in silence.

Then, Lady Stone placed her fingers against his arm. A heady effect, one that stirred him in places he dared not name. Visceral desire joined his extraordinary response to her pain.

He struggled to master his need as he followed the course she chose. Anyone looking would have assumed he led, but he'd known men with less determined strides, less mettle, less pride.

She did not speak. Her silence did not matter. Remaining close was his only concern. Close enough for her scent to permeate less alluring smells. Close enough to feel the rise and fall of her shoulders.

When they reached the corner just beyond her street, she stopped.

"Thank you, sir, for your kindness." She released his arm, and bowed her head. "We will make our way from here."

Chev's warning wrangled with Ash's ferocious need until reluctantly, he agreed. If he were to spirit her away, what then? He had nothing to give. Nothing that would staunch the flow of her pain.

"I will wait here until you are safely inside," he said.

Her companion turned away. She nodded before following. As they rounded the corner, she glanced back.

That gesture was his undoing.

Intentionally or not, she'd opened a window into her essence, and he'd seen a mirror of his own.

She'd left the country of her youth, she'd been cast off, heartbroken, and yet, she retained a natural sincerity, purer than anything he'd ever known.

He did not, in fact, have anything to give. And she was, as warned, embroiled in scandal enough without him.

It did not matter. They must meet again, and soon. His life depended on a closer acquaintance. A *much* closer acquaintance.

CHAPTER 4

*A*sh's fortnight of planning had finally met its moment of truth. His eyes adjusted to the dim light of the alleyway. No sign marked the entrance of the small establishment known as Marie's, but rare was the hot-blooded male unaware of its existence. Marie and her women stitched sinfully silky concoctions, chiefly for the celebrated members of London's demimonde, the half-strata of society occupied by mistresses and actors, divorced wives, and poets.

A buffed-brass shop bell trilled as Ash entered.

This wasn't Ash's first visit. Madame Bianci wouldn't have been caught dead in undergarments made from anyone else. Ash esteemed Marie as a talented tradeswoman—discreet, with an ingenious understanding of texture and design. However, when he'd hired a man to uncover places he might 'accidentally' discover Lady Stone, Marie's had been the last place he'd expected to find his mark.

His man paid a shop girl for answers. The answers provided Ash his opportunity.

For years, idle Tuesdays had strung together, providing no change but the ever-deepening wrinkles in his skin. For a time, idle days had been a comfort. However, on this idle Tuesday—at around quarter-past six—his life would transform once again.

Provided she agreed to his proposition, of course.

He'd crafted his impending offer with great intention. A liaison, brief enough to ensure he did not bring harm to Lady Stone, and long enough for him to absorb the light she had to offer.

He was alive with anticipation.

Marie arrived in the elegantly appointed sitting area. Her reserved expression broke into a genuine smile when she recognized Ash.

"Ah. Your Grace."

"Marie." He took her hands in his, leaned down and kissed her on each cheek.

A curtsey from her would have been appropriate, but no one stood on ceremony here. Marie's concoctions might as well have been stitched with the scandalous secrets of half the peerage.

"What brings you today?" Her sly eyes met his. "Has Madame Bianci grown tired of her last dressing gown so soon?"

"My dear Marie," he smiled, "I am certain you know Miss White has transferred her affections."

Her eyes went wide with innocence. "Surely, you intend to fight for the lady's love! May I suggest a gift, perhaps, to prove your sweet devotion?"

"Alas," Ash held a hand to his heart, "when the prima donna met the Russian prince a fortnight ago, I hear it was love, prima facie. I am afraid there is nothing I can do."

"Well." Madame arched a brow. "I cannot blame Madame Bianci. A woman likes to be wanted."

Ash should have been insulted. His cold reserve, however, was legendary. And, she was right. Women yearned to be wanted. *He* yearned to be wanted.

A yearning that had never been truly satisfied.

"Water under the bridge, Marie. I wish the newly minted couple *souchastiye*."

Marie lifted one shoulder in an uncaring shrug, but the knowing did not fade from her gaze. "You have come for a reason, *non*?"

"I am here to buy the debt of the late Admiral Stone."

Marie's start revealed her surprise. She recovered quickly. "If you are looking to obtain the graces of the countess, paying the admiral's debts will do no such thing. The countess has sworn never to look at another man."

"I've heard." Ash returned her knowing gaze. "I've also heard the countess is in debt to every shopkeeper in London. And being an excellent businesswoman, you undoubtedly sought relief elsewhere." He adjusted a mirror atop the counter so he could keep one eye on the door. "I have it on good authority that his widow is expected here within the hour. Lady Stone comes, I understand, quarterly. Always on a Tuesday, between six and half-past. She leaves without making a purchase."

"Perhaps I have *sought relief*." Marie's mouth pinched. "Silks are not free, your grace."

"No, indeed." He inclined his head. "Nor have you any reason for raised hackles. Your collection strategies are none of my concern. I am offering to pay the admiral's debt."

"And in return?"

"A quarter hour of privacy in your dressing room. I wish to speak with Lady Stone."

Marie's eyes went wide.

"I intend nothing untoward." At least not here. Not yet. "I wish only to personally express my condolences."

Marie's expression cleared. "If you wish it, it will be done."

"My thanks." A mask of indifference concealed the pace of his heart.

He was So. Damn. Close.

"I will send the admiral's bill to your secretary."

"You needn't mark it as the admiral's debt."

"Of course not, Your Grace." Marie's eyelids swept down.

"This way to the dressing room, if you please."

PAYING debts Octavius had accrued in pursuit of the countess was an unfair burden, but watching the balances decrease gave Alicia a sense of satisfaction. She'd always suspected Octavius's accusation that *she* overspent had been false. Now she had proof. She could economize. She hadn't much, and, if the countess took the income from Octavius's estates, she'd have even less, but she had proven she could live within her means. And she could do it while decreasing *his* debt.

Her freedom had been hard-won—the expense, Octavius's life. Octavius had only been thinking of his country, of course, but she vowed not to take his sacrifice for granted.

She thought of the funeral procession and shivered.

She did not wish to think of that day. She especially did not wish to think of the handsome stranger who had witnessed her at her most vulnerable, and then offered his assistance.

She silenced her thoughts and concentrated on following Madame Marie to her dressing room. For the first time since she'd begun making payments, Marie had requested she wait. A gossip-inclined client was to arrive any moment, Marie explained. Lady Stone did not wish to make known her husband's debts. And, of course, her presence could only cause speculation.

Alicia reluctantly agreed.

"I will be with you as soon as possible." The modiste hesitated, her gaze moved toward the far end of the room. "And if you need anything, I will hear you call."

Alicia frowned at Madame's back. Curious to be asked to wait, and more curious still, to insinuate she may need assistance.

She set down her reticule and unbuttoned her coat, glancing askance at the red velvet couch and then around the room.

Multiple hooks lined burgundy walls adorned with mirrors reflecting every angle. The opposite of the room contained an over-large privacy screen.

She rolled her shoulders, discomfited by the blatant eroticism. Truthfully, the room reminded her of a brothel. Though she'd never been inside a brothel, her small island had its share of those who lived and loved on the wrong side of propriety.

The most successful had resided together in a house with windows that looked out to the sea. When a ship came in, they donned ill-fitting gowns far too outrageous for their corner of the world before welcoming wave-weary men into their rooms. Some nights, as Alicia passed by in the shadows, she heard sounds of laughter and lust.

Oh, she knew those ladies' lives were not all gaiety. Sometimes children came months after the ship had departed. Sometimes disease.

But still, the sounds coming through windows open to the night breeze were sounds of pleasure. Whenever she heard such sounds, she'd been rendered curious and hot, imagining what her first time would be like.

What a terrible disappointment the marriage bed had been.

Octavius preferred his wife to remain quiet, still, and fully clothed. In fact, he'd been adamant that anything else would fail to keep her pure. Judging from the scandalous concoctions hanging from the hooks, he'd expected something far different from the countess.

She reached out to finger a dressing gown. *Heavenly.* And the color! Pink. Not just any pink, but rose, light as an innocent's blush. She placed her hand beneath the fabric. Even in the low light, the fabric was so thin she could make out the lines in the crook of her hand. Octavius's voice seemed to travel through the years. *...There's an M in your right hand. That means you will be married.*

How could someone who wooed with such romance thoroughly shatter her heart? He'd been the perfect gentleman. And she'd wanted to be the perfect wife. Then, he'd found the perfect mistress.

She dropped the dressing gown. For a respectable widow, the cost of freedom was lifelong celibacy. Anything sensual and soft was none of her concern.

The door closed, followed quickly by the groan of a lock.

A distinctly male scent filled the air—*wealthy* male, a scent she recognized but could not place. The hair on her neck raised; she forced a calming breath. Nothing came of panic. She'd learned that on the high seas.

"Please, have a seat."

His cultured intonation disproved her first assumption—that he was yet another of Octavius's creditors, the horrid men who demanded money in the most unlikely of places.

"Imprisonment," she said coolly, refusing to turn, "is not to my taste. And if it is not to yours, I suggest you unlock that door."

"Admirable restraint," he said.

"Losing one's head is a luxury afforded only to those accustomed to care."

He made a deep, humming sort of sound, a sound she felt in her belly.

"A woman such as yourself *should* be accustomed to care."

She added outrageous to a list that included male, wealthy, and cultured. "I do not believe we've been introduced, Mr.—?"

"The honorific you seek is Your Grace."

She turned. His face was illuminated by the faint glow spilling from a lighted sconce.

The duke—if he was truly a duke—was at least a full head taller than she, but it was his smoldering eyes that sparked recognition. He was the man from the funeral.

For a split second that might as well have been an eternity, her mind went blessedly blank. Then, bereft of thought's direction, her senses began to dance.

Stop, she ordered.

But he smells so nice, they whined.

"You've surmised you are in no immediate danger."

But she *was* in danger. Pure peril, actually—past, present and future. "Have I surmised correctly?"

Smile was not the right word for what happened to his mouth. A smile stood for camaraderie or at the very least, amusement. His lips, ever so slightly upturned, were entirely predatorial.

She should have known better than to accept his help, even if she had judged him altruistic. Nothing good came from depending on a man.

"Won't you sit?" he asked before taking a seat himself.

He'd left her little choice—to remain standing was to disrespect his station. Although if society's rules governed this situation, she'd be heartily astonished. She settled onto the couch by his side, their knees mere inches apart.

"You are correct. Your person is not," he paused, "at this moment, in danger."

Then why was her heart beating like a rabbit hiding in brush? "I am relieved, Your Grace."

His right eyebrow shot up. "Sarcasm does not become you."

She narrowed her eyes. "If my tone disrespects, you might look to your actions."

He made a sound of disappointment. "Have I accosted you?"

She glanced sideways at his hands. "No."

"Treated you poorly?"

"I would define undeserved imprisonment as poor treatment."

"You are free to go." He stretched out a leg. "If that is your wish."

"You locked the door."

"To keep others out, not to keep you in."

Her gaze flicked to the door. "Is there a reason you wish to speak with me?"

"I, too, appreciate economy of conversation. I shall come to my point. As a gift to you, on behalf of a grateful nation, I have paid your husband's debt to Marie."

It was a good thing she had been clenching her teeth, else her jaw would have dropped.

"—And the apothecary—"

She sucked in. That was Aunt Hester's debt!

"—And the jeweler—"

"Why?" The question burst forth.

"Charity." He paused to flick a non-existent piece of lint from his trousers. "Or incentive...whichever you prefer."

She stood.

"Please." It was a command—

"Please?"—a command she did not heed.

"I've thought of little but you since..." he stopped himself.

"Have you?" So strange to be looking down at a duke. "I don't see why. I am entirely forgettable."

"How *very* wrong you are. I've gone through a great deal of trouble just to ensure we met again."

She frowned. "Do you expect me to be flattered?"

"Some would be."

She snorted. "I doubt your understanding of the fairer sex."

"I'll admit to limited experience." He smiled again, still slight, and this time with regret.

"Does this limited experience include the expectation that any woman you attend will just..." She could not say it aloud.

"You needn't assume the worst. When I discovered the particulars of your situation, as a gentleman, I could not stand idly by while a lady assumed debts rightfully belonging to—."

"Stop." The room swayed. It was one thing for all of England to know your husband spent extravagant sums on someone else. It was quite another to have a stranger lay bare your pain.

"I only meant to point out," he said, "the debt never truly belonged to you, thus payment cannot make you beholden."

She took a deep breath. The duke would never understand that he'd taken the only thing that had provided her a sense of ascendency over her humiliation. Worse still, he *had* left her beholden to him, whether he had intended to or not.

"What is it you wish of me?"

"Do you prefer I be blunt?"

She nodded.

His eyes glittered. "I would like to bed you."

She lost her voice. Instinctively, her hand flew to her throat. But other parts of her—parts that had been in long slumber, were suddenly awake. Awake and shamelessly attuned to the duke.

"But," he continued, "I would like you to come to my bed of your own free will."

Indecent images of sheets and pillows and tangled limbs filled her mind. An earthquake shook her boxed longing, releasing chaos that would have made Pandora blush.

She closed her eyes and concentrated. "You want *me*...in a carnal sense?"

"Is that so hard to believe?"

Yes. She made the mistake of challenging him with a direct gaze. His conversation may have been urbane, but his eyes were the eyes of a desperate man—a haunted man. She didn't have that kind of power. Did she?

Feminine laughter echoed through her memory. Laughter spilling from rooms with windows left wide to the moonlight, interspersed with cries of *yes* and *please* and *more*.

"You've paid my late husband's debts because you want me."

"No," he said. "I paid the debt out of respect. I used the subsequent opportunity to meet you." He strung out the silence as if he were unraveling a knot. "And I wanted to meet you"—he leaned forward—"because I want you in my bed."

Was this how dukes behaved? Plucking marks from crowds, luring them into dark spaces and then proposing wicked things?

Wicked things that inspired heaviness in her breasts and

aching in her groin. Strange sensations that ought to have sent her running for the door.

But she was not running for the door, like she ought.

She was not calling for Marie, like she ought.

Heaven help her, she was concealing a watering mouth.

The duke exuded the promise of pleasure she had never known, but had always longed to experience. And, he was offering her that pleasure without ties.

Tempted did not begin to describe her state.

BECAUSE I WANT *you in my bed*. The words stung his throat.

He hadn't meant to state his need in such crude terms. Hell, he hadn't even slept in his bed since the fire. Sleep, when it came, was little more than a few quiet hours, leaning back in a soft chair. When he pictured Lady Stone, however, she was definitely in his bed. At Wisterley. A bed he'd never occupied with anyone else.

His words had caused her distress.

He was a terrible man. But he'd known that for some time. He wanted her anyway.

He'd been intrigued by Chev's description. Then transfixed by a single glimpse. And now that he'd seen her lower lip tremble in want of his kiss, nothing in hell, heaven, or earth could stand in his way.

"I cannot," she said.

Nothing but her conscience, anyway.

"Why not?" he asked.

Her mouth opened and then closed. "Well, there are moral consid—"

"To hell with morality."

Her eyebrows shot up. "Hell is exactly my concern."

He snorted. "You are a widow. If we are discreet—and I am

always discreet—no one of consequence will know."

"*I* will know."

He studied her face. "I cannot offer you the sanctity of marriage, if there is such a thing as sanctity."

A look of horror passed over her features. "I did not mean...that is to say, I would never be so bold to suggest marriage to a duke." She recovered her composure. "Especially one who wishes to make me his plaything."

Plaything? His brows shot up. "I do not play."

"You want me to be your mistress."

"No," he replied. "I want you in my bed for three nights. That is all I ask."

She blinked. "Pardon?"

He smoothed a crease in his trousers. "I am not at liberty to provide an extended liaison." Any longer would leave her burned. At best, desolate and weeping, like Liza. At worst...

He wouldn't consider the worst.

Her breath caused her shoulders to rise and fall. They were approaching something. What, he hadn't any idea.

"I am intrigued," she replied, finally. "And tempted, shamed as I am to admit it. But I cannot"—she flushed scarlet—"grant your wish."

"Tempted," he murmured.

She turned her back, and her features were reflected in the mirror by the door. He stood up, framing her with his body.

"We make a handsome couple, don't you think?" He grasped her shoulders. "An intriguing contrast of light and dark."

Her eyes were cocked pistols, following every move. "You frighten me, Duke."

"Truly, you have no cause to fear. I am at your mercy."

Her lips parted.

"I will," he lowered his voice, "obey *any* command."

She did not ask him to step away.

"I would like to remove your hat," he said. "May I?"

"Why?" she asked.

"Because I long to touch your hair." He moved his right hand to her chin, accidentally skimming her breasts with his arm. Blood drained to his groin. "You brush your hair every night, don't you? As if in preparation for a lover."

She nodded, seemingly transfixed by their reflection.

"I want to be that lover," he whispered.

She whimpered. Then, her weapon-eyes returned to his. "Only my hat? You promise?"

"Yes." For now.

"Very well."

So prim. So proper. Soon, he'd coax open those tight little lips, and urge them to speak very improper things.

He pulled the string securing her bonnet. Her hat tumbled to the ground. He held her from behind, leaving one hand where the ribbon had been tied, and resting the other lightly on her hip.

He inhaled her scent as he swept his cheek from her crown to her ear. Her hair was smooth, but it had been stretched, twisted, and pinned into a bun far too severe for her face. He longed to free her locks. He also longed to stretch and twist and pin her in other ways, to make his sheets a canvas, and her body, the art.

But even if she did agree to his proposal, he would not subject his angel to his most prurient desires. She deserved his best.

He brushed a few fallen strands of hair from her neck. While holding her gaze in the mirror, he touched his lips to the flesh above her shoulder. Her shudder passed from her body to his. She moaned, a sound like water on parched clay.

"Shh," he crooned.

Gently, he urged her to relax against his chest. Her weight was every bit as exhilarating as he'd hoped. He kissed her on her crown and cradled her close. Then, intentionally, she rubbed her cheek against his arm.

He hardened further.

He *would* have her, even if he must swear she would be the last woman whose body he'd ever worship.

"You have had the marriage without the sanctity," he spoke against her skin. "If you insist, I will offer you the sanctity without the marriage."

"What do you mean?" Breathless.

"I cannot," he paused to correct himself, "I *will* not marry again. But if you come to me, I will promise you fidelity, even after we part."

She met his eyes in the mirror. "Devil," she accused.

He nodded. "I have been told I dwell in darkness." Her scent was blossoming gardens and light. "And I think, love, that you wish to join me, if only for a time." His fingers caressed her hip. "Permission. That's all it will cost."

With a rush of hot breath, she turned in his embrace. "I want to say yes, but I cannot."

Her lips were saying one thing. Her eyes, something else.

"When you come to my bed, I will touch you in any way you wish to be touched, kiss you every place you wish to be kissed." The pressure in his balls intensified. "I ask only three nights, after which you may return to your world, reputation intact."

"*I* will know," she repeated, this time in a whisper.

"Yes, you will know," he replied. "And I swear you will never forget."

He resisted the overwhelming urge to claim her lips.

First, she must agree.

"Passion for three nights," he said. "Fidelity forever."

He meant the promise with all that was left of his ravaged heart.

What did it matter if he never coupled again? He'd sacrifice anything for her intimate touch. For a look of sensual wonder on her face. For the chance to find that too-brief oblivion and shudder helplessly in her embrace.

"Your Grace—"

"Ashbey. Ash, if you wish."

Her fingers cut into his arms. "I am deeply sorry, *Your Grace*, but I cannot. I want to, but I cannot. You have placed me in your debt, and to acquiesce now..." She shook her head no. "I can't. It would not be right."

The power in his body coalesced. *Take her anyway. That is what she really wants.* He silenced the command. Passion—true passion —came only as a gift.

He used every ounce of his willpower to step away from the comfort of her heat. "You are making a mistake."

"No," she countered. "Though I am certain I will regret my decision."

"Regret," he repeated, "is a bitter pill."

"So is loss."

Loss? He frowned. "I would take nothing from you."

"You would take my most valued possession—my self-respect."

"Fidelity forever. I do not make promises I cannot keep." He could see he would not prevail if he persisted. Not tonight. He retrieved her hat. "When you change your mind, send word through Marie."

She hung her reticule on her wrist. Its tassels danced as he retied the ribbon. She was trembling from head to toe.

Good.

He unlocked and opened the door.

"Duke," she acknowledged with a nod.

"Lady Stone." He bowed.

She held her breath, and then turned to stride through the shop. At the door, she paused.

If she looked back, he would win.

The bell trilled.

With one hand still on the handle, she glanced over her shoulder. And then, she sighed.

The serpent inside him coiled, in preparation for the proper time to strike.

CHAPTER 5

*A*licia's virtue would have had a fighting chance...if the Admiralty had not mistakenly sent her the countess's letters.

The packet had been waiting when she returned from Marie's. A packet full of sheaves addressed to Octavius from the countess. And a single, unfinished letter, addressed to the countess and written in Octavius's familiar hand.

A wiser woman would have left the packet untouched.

The words within the letters were not meant for her eyes. Even Octavius would never have been so cruel. She read them nonetheless—line after excruciating line, pulsing with love that was somehow both prurient and pure. Mutual joy lived within the lines, between them, even—reverence for each other's bodies, infinite respect for each other's souls, and a solemn commitment to the child their love had delivered into this world.

Alicia passed a finger over Octavius's signature, hearing the words of the vicious patron—*the countess would have made the admiral the perfect wife if the barren shrew he married had the grace to die.*

She nearly choked.

The whole world thought her worthless. The young woman had wished her dead. She dropped the letter onto her bed. She was, as she'd always been, unwanted.

Though not entirely.

Not anymore.

One duke, one dangerous, possibly mad and devastatingly handsome duke, had sworn a lifetime of celibacy in exchange for three nights in her arms.

He tried to buy you using Octavius's debt. But hadn't he also given her a glimpse of passion, sublime?

If she agreed, they would enter into a wicked accounting she abhorred. She'd become *a lover.* A person who indulged in pleasures never meant to be theirs.

On the other hand, who would she harm? She was betraying no one.

Yes, she had vowed to protect her freedom, but the duke hadn't asked for her autonomy. He'd asked for her permission.

Heaven, did she wish to grant him that. How she longed to know passion.

She'd known he was hot and hard from the time he'd taken her into his arms. *For her.* Not for someone else he imagined when he closed his eyes.

She'd been tempted.

Not just tempted. *Convinced.*

She might argue reasons—valid reasons—but the truth was, she'd refused mostly out of fear.

She was afraid no longer. She'd had enough of being on the outside looking in. Everyone else indulged without compunction. Why couldn't she? Just for three nights?

The very next morning, she visited Marie, delivering a note with her terms. Anonymity. No lasting ties. The morning after that, she received directions.

Aunt Hester, to her surprise, had accepted that she'd been summoned by a relation of her father's. Hester's protest had been minimal at best. She did not like to travel and her coterie of gossiping friends were due to arrive for their usual weekly tea on the morrow.

Alicia departed, per his instructions, in the crestless carriage he'd sent. The curtains remained tightly drawn as the carriage rambled through so many twists and turns, she could have been anywhere in England.

Anywhere within a half-day's ride of London, anyway.

She only ventured to look out the window when the coachman abruptly stopped. A sheep, he explained, had become entangled in the prickly blackthorn brush lining the drive, and they could not pass without mounting a rescue.

"Them at the castle don't keep it trimmed the way they used to," he complained.

Indeed, the hedgerow seemed wild, twisted, and menacing, though not nearly as menacing as the castle tower at the top of the hill, half shrouded by clouds and half eerily-outlined by the moon.

"That's where we're headed," the coachman said. "Unless you wish to turn back."

A castle. Of course, the duke would have a castle.

When they reached the entry, she placed her fingers into the coachman's hand and slid inelegantly from his grace's carriage. Her walking boots hit gravel, and, simultaneously, the tower lit from the sky with unholy light. A crack of thunder followed, sounding like a coachman's whip.

Aptly impressive welcome, devil duke.

Ashbey's power had felt supernatural from the first. His timing, eerie. But—she inhaled—any lingering disquiet was nothing more than fancy born of a long ride in a closed, curtained carriage. The only power the duke possessed was the power she granted.

Correction.

The duke did not have power over *her* beyond the power she

granted. Of course, a duke had power enough to appear super-natural to a mere mortal like herself.

She must remind herself he was a man. Flesh and blood like any other. If, perhaps, more gifted in the flesh.

Lucky for her.

She survived the marl with minimal damage to her shoes, and faced the forbidding oak doors, waiting for the coachman to heft the iron knocker. Her gaze slid to the coachman. Did he believe the lie her clothing conveyed: that she was a housekeeper, come to be interviewed?

Doubtful.

The door swung open. Light from a fire in the great hall silhouetted an aging servant. With exaggerated motions, he ushered her inside.

"Wait here, ma'am."

Without even an unspoken offer to remove her sodden cloak, the servant disappeared.

She wasn't ready to relinquish the thick, woolen garment anyway, even if rain drops glistened between its fibers. Damp-ness clung to the stone walls, making the chill on the inside nearly worse than outside. The flames leaping in the giant hearth did little to tame the shadows or ease the cold. Surprisingly, her teeth did not chatter.

Lud, but the place was old. She would have expected *some* modification. She glanced up into the darkened rafters. Some-thing squeaked.

Bats?

She scowled and took a step closer to the hearth. Disem-bodied voices echoed against the walls. She tilted her head, but could not discern a single word.

If she released the reins on her imagination, she could fancy herself transported back in time, a medieval vassal awaiting the Lord of the Manor. Doubtless, such fancies would serve the duke's purpose. No matter how indebted she felt, she was no helpless maid to his feudal lord.

The duke appeared on the stair, his face cloaked by shadow. "You came."

She moistened her lips. "Did you ever doubt, Your Grace? This was all impressively planned."

He stepped into the hall. He wore no cravat and his linen shirt fell open at his throat, making her feel as if she had already sinned. She forced her gaze up from the indecent exposure of flesh. Heat crept into her cheeks.

"Let us not begin on a lie," he said. "Admit you are here of your own free will, or go."

"Do you deny that you placed me in your debt?"

"Charity, of course," he replied. "It is your choice to perceive obligation. I'll not take a martyr into my bed."

"As always, you are very direct."

"Do you disapprove?"

"No." She liked the way he spoke—free of embarrassment or disdain. In fact, it stole her breath. "I find prevarication of little use. I am here. Three days I have promised, three days I will give."

"Nights, my lady." His tenor warmed.

Her usual distaste for *my lady* failed. The words became honey on his lips—smooth, rich, and sweet.

He clasped his hands behind his back, slowly circling her. "*Nights* at the mercy of both your passions"—his lids veiled his gaze—"and mine."

"Oh *my*." She longed to be at his mercy, and she longed to have him at hers.

He chuckled, a sound at odds with the dungeon-like surroundings.

She bent a knee, and inclined her head in a short, swift mockery of a curtsey. "Three nights you have, Your Grace. I trust you have kept your end of the bargain."

"The three servants present have not been given your name.

You've met the coachman and Kent. The final is a woman, who will serve as cook and lady's maid. I assure you, they are loyal and discreet. There will be no lasting ties."

She closed her eyes and exhaled.

"Have you any remaining limitations that would prevent you from enjoying what is to come?" he asked.

Irony she did not appreciate laced through his words. She looked him in the eye. She wanted him, yes. But a spade should be called a spade.

"I am sorry," she said with sarcasm. "Did you assume I would have no difficulty agreeing to become your whore?"

He was silent for too long, and something dark lurked behind his gaze. "Such an ugly word," he said finally, "from such pretty lips."

"If not a whore, what am I?"

"You are—" He stopped abruptly and blinked, as if his instinctive answer had caused him surprise.

Had she not been so desperate to know what he'd kept silent, she would have cheered the small win. Instead, she shivered.

"Forgive me." He recovered. "I should have offered to take your cloak. You are soaking."

He unclasped the hooks at her throat, lifted the cloak from her shoulders and then dropped it onto the wet stone floor.

She sighed. "You've ruined it, no doubt."

"I will buy you another." His gaze grew speculative. "A cloak lined with sable, perhaps."

She lifted her brows. "Sable would be warm, certainly."

"It could be yours. If..." His voice trailed.

She narrowed her eyes. "If?"

"If you are good." He stepped close enough for her to feel his heat against the exposed skin above her fichu. He brought his lips next to her ear. "And you will be good, won't you, love?"

"I am afraid I am at a loss, Your Grace."

He cupped her cheek. "I'd be happy to be of help."

"How does the Duke of Ashbey define *good*? Because I suspect you are not referring to virtue."

He smiled, dark and wolfish. "Just admit you are here of your own free will so we may proceed."

His radiating heat made her dizzy. Her dependably sturdy legs quivered. "I thought I had."

"Not quite."

His face was blurred, his lips impossibly close, and his scent, an invitation to indulge in her most dissipated needs. Again, she remembered the old wives' tale: Demons could not be summoned without express request.

To hell with cloaks and banter.

"Yes," she replied. "I am here of my own free will."

His ragged sigh gave her chills. "Then let us set aside questions of virtue."

"Devil," she whispered.

"I am," he said, with all seriousness. "But I am also a devil you desire."

What was the point of denial? "Yes."

"The truth at last." He stepped away. "There is a bath prepared. Warm yourself. And be ready." He pulled the bell and within seconds the old butler appeared. "Kent, would you lead the lady to my chamber?"

She followed the servant up the stairs, feeling the duke's gaze fixed upon her clinging skirts.

THE DUKE OF ASHBEY might have been a libidinous youth for all the dignity he'd just displayed. His most valued possessions had been consigned to flame. Now he'd lost one of the few remaining things he prized—his self-discipline.

Resting his forehead against the smooth wooden door that led to the dressing room, he listened. Her sigh throbbed in his weighted cock.

He gripped the doorframe, tensing his muscles as if he could physically resist his need. His desire taunted, urging him to take his manhood into his hand and stroke until he spent.

But he would not waste his arousal.

He would have his angel soon enough. They would come together in the messy ritual belonging not to Heaven, nor to Hades, but to earth—slow, deliberate, thorough, and *real*. He would savor all her luscious curves, and then sink into her as if she were solace personified. And for the time they came together, he'd be cleansed of the past and its pain.

He closed his eyes, reliving the very first time he had laid eyes on Lady Stone.

He'd come back to life. There was no other way to describe the quickening. Resurrection, but incomplete. Solitude had never bothered him, but he'd been shrinking away from the land of the living for too long when their moment of connection had brought him back with a rush of pain and a deluge of desire.

He craved more. She could give him more. And she would.

He'd paid dearly for the woman.

He swatted away a sudden surge of guilt. She'd said she was here of her own free will. Was that not enough to muzzle his conscience?

Through the wood he heard the murmuring of female conversation. He'd been surprised Mrs. Kent had agreed to travel back to the ruins of Wisterley, not just because of the questionable moral nature of the journey, but because the castle was said to be cursed. Kent, of course, had never been afraid.

Ashbey refused to dwell any longer on the rumors that clung to the castle, nor would he allow himself to consider the wing he'd never rebuilt, but instead left to char and ruin. He was here, at Wisterley. For the first time since the fire, he was anticipating a night within the castle.

And the tingle in his balls? The one that filled him with glee (Yes—devil take it—*glee*)? That was a sensation he hadn't felt since he'd been young and ruttish and blind to his future tribulations.

He turned his attention back to the woman within Wisterley's oldest and only undamaged tower. Inside the dressing room, the water swished.

He imagined her standing in the copper tub, bare as Venus. More likely, she had retained her shift. She was proper that way.

So proper he could not wait to spread her thighs.

It would now be up to him to ensure she was properly, thoroughly satisfied.

And he was fully 'up' to the task.

CHAPTER 6

A woman who'd given her name as Mrs. Kent had appeared, offering to assist Alicia with her bath. Mrs. Kent was so full of youth and vigor, when the young woman confided that she was married to the much older butler, Alicia failed to mask her surprise.

Alicia apologized immediately.

"Go on." Mrs. Kent waved her hand. "You aren't the first to give us the eye. The difference in age 'tisn't anybody's concern but ours, is it? He makes me laugh and"—she winked—"he's a right bit better in the ways that concern us women than my first husband, rest his soul."

First husband.

As she bathed, she tested and discarded the phrase. 'Admiral Octavius Stone, my *first* husband,' implied there would be a next. She may long to experience passion, but no man alive could convince her to become his bride.

Enough certainly was enough, thank you very much.

After helping Alicia towel dry, Mrs. Kent lifted a fresh shift over Alicia's head. The fabric slithered down over her curves gentler than a whisper.

"Linen?" she asked.

"Yes, linen," Mrs. Kent answered. "Soft, 'tisn't it? I never saw the like." She leaned back and squinted. "Did I do it right?"

Alicia straightened the gown. "Perfect, as far as I'm concerned."

Mrs. Kent began collecting the towels. "I'm afraid I've never played lady's maid before."

Laughter bubbled up in Alicia's throat. Fear, she supposed. Fear or hysteria.

"Are you well?" Mrs. Kent asked.

Alicia nodded. "It's just that you didn't hesitate to use the word lady."

Mrs. Kent squinted one eye. "You're quality, anyone can see that." She shrugged. "Mr. Kent don't judge, and neither do I. Besides, the duke's come back to Wisterley. Been an age. Your doin', I think. That's quite something, indeed."

With those astonishing words, Mrs. Kent took her leave.

The duke came back? Where had he been?

Alicia wrapped her arms about her waist. The room was as ancient as the entry hall, decorated by intricately carved, dark wood panels. Thick velvet curtains blocked out the storm beyond. The room's single inviting feature was the bed.

She touched the dressing gown lying across the mattress. The fabric was pale pink and somehow familiar. She ran her hand over the fabric. *Silk.* Not just silk but silk so finely woven, it spilled through her fingers like water.

Then she remembered. This was the dressing gown she'd been admiring at Marie's.

Ah. The duke wasn't a devil. He was an equally dangerous kind of being—the kind of man who noticed, the kind who remembered.

The kind who made a lady's wishes come true.

She slipped into the dressing gown. The fire in her belly was anticipation come to tingling life. This was wrong. All of this, wrong.

And yet so sinfully right.

Cloaked in a fine linen shift and then wrapped in a luxurious silken robe, she warred inwardly between uncertainty and anticipation. If the duke did not appear soon, she feared uncertainty would win. Then, she would run from the room screaming like a madwoman.

Or she could choose to behave with her usual practiced composure and calmly take a seat. She sat on the mattress, though the posture did little to strengthen her calm.

She glanced over at the table. Mrs. Kent had left a few slices of cheese, bread, and a steaming cup of—she leaned forward and sniffed—chocolate. Tempting as the chocolate was, how was she to eat or drink when she could barely swallow?

A knock at the door made her jump.

"Come in." Had that been her voice, all satin and invitation? Good heavens, if a mere hour in this place had brought on that change, what would she sound like at the end of three days?

Nights, my lady.

She shuddered, first from the memory of his words and then from the reality of his physical presence.

He entered wearing an outrageous golden dressing gown looking more like a Grecian god than a proper English peer. Only his throat was fully exposed, but his Adam's apple was enough to leave her transfixed.

He rested his gaze on her lips. She curved them into a shape she hoped resembled a smile. Without returning the expression, he sauntered forward and placed a finger under her chin.

"If you're trying to appear welcoming, you can do better."

"I'm afraid not," she said. "I wish I could."

His gaze slid to the sideboard. "You haven't so much as nibbled."

"I am too unsettled to eat."

"A drink, then, at least?"

She shook her head no. "The chocolate is too hot."

"Try this." He handed her a glass she had not noticed.

She accepted with lifted brows.

"Brandy," he answered her unspoken question.

Octavius had disapproved of ladies who drank spirits.

But Octavius was not present, was he? He'd never have the power to control her behavior again.

Tentatively, she sipped. A taste like summer's heat burned down her throat. Berries—cherry, currant, raspberry, and a hint of spice—all things opposite the dark, wild wind beyond the window.

She warmed from the inside out.

"Delicious." She briefly closed her eyes.

He joined her on the bed. She swallowed another sip and what was left of her pride.

"What next?" If her breath came any faster, tears might follow.

He tilted his head. "We haven't discussed protections."

"Protections?"

"I have a wrapper."

She frowned.

"The kind used to prevent pregnancy," he explained.

Her lips formed an O. "That doesn't sound..."

"Comfortable?" he offered. "It is not."

"There is—" She bit her lip hard enough to induce pain before glancing away. Hadn't the duke heard the woman on the day of the procession? She was barren. "There is no need for precaution. I was married for eight years and did not bear a child."

"If you are certain, I'd gladly forgo the precaution."

Her brow creased. "Certain?"

"Perhaps," he replied carefully, "the fault was not yours."

"Please do not mock me." She drew her legs upward, her posture as much an outward display of protection as it was an inward defense.

He ducked to catch her eye. "I would never mock you."

She glared in accusation. "You *know* the countess bore my late husband's child."

"I know the admiral *claimed* a child. Neither of us, I believe, are privy to the exact circumstances of the child's birth."

She stiffened. "Are you implying Octavia is not his?"

"Are you offended on behalf of your husband's mistress?"

"Not on her behalf." Again, she looked away. On behalf of love, she supposed. Only a deep, abiding, and—yes—*faithful* love could have caused Octavius to humiliate his family as he had. No one could convince her otherwise.

And Octavia was an innocent, born into circumstances beyond her control.

The duke brushed aside her hair with gentle fingers. "Come back to me."

"I have not left," she huffed.

"Your husband should have desired you."

"He did." Her lip quivered. "In his way."

The duke leaned forward, surprising her by placing the lightest of kisses against her mouth. Their first kiss, she realized with shock. His lips were warm, dry and infinitely tender. Tender, yes, but potent enough to vanquish thoughts of Octavius. From the moment they'd touched, every inch of her body had lit from within.

"Breathe," he commanded.

Air entered her chest in a rush. Her inexperience became painfully clear. She was rabbit to his hawk, no matter how gentle his touch.

"I've never spoken to anyone else about"—she felt her cheeks heat—"my husband's infidelity. With you, I am not myself. I speak of things that shame me. I acquiesce to things that surprise me. I *detest* the power you have over me."

He did not seem perturbed. "You needn't feel shame—not

with me. And I've been told power is considered by some to be an ancient aphrodisiac."

Was it? She had not been drawn to the duke because of his title.

She hadn't even known he possessed a title at first. She'd been drawn to him because of the way he'd looked at her—as if she mattered, as if he understood.

He traced a lazy line up her arm before resting his hand on her shoulder. Her heart beat in a jagged rhythm, half terror and half anticipation—Persephone waking to discover she had been taken, against her will, to the underworld. Although, unlike Persephone, she had willingly entered the duke's lair.

Ashbey represented darkness and heat and all things forbidden, and she wanted him with a power strong enough to stamp out both her reason and her virtue. Once before, she had done everything as she should. Misery had been the result. This time, she would do everything she ought not, and perhaps—

Perhaps what?

What was the unspoken wish inside her heart?

"You've disappeared again." His voice soothed.

"You frighten me," she said.

"Describe your fear."

"Is it not obvious?"

"No." He shifted positions so that he rested his weight on his elbow. "Where does your fear reside?"

She kept her eyes from rolling. "You know how fear feels, Duke."

"Do I?" He tilted his head. "Perhaps I did, once. Humor me."

She frowned. "My chest is constricted."

"How?"

Her frown deepened. "As if I were still wearing stays."

"Breathe," he reminded again. "And go on."

Why did she feel like a bug, pinned for examination? "I fear what you will do next and yet"—breathe—"my heartbeat pounds when I feel your touch."

He placed her closed palm against his cheek. Reflexively, she opened her hand. The flesh beneath her fingers was rough with stubble.

Rough and warm.

"If yours is an apt description," he said, "then *I* am not afraid."

"*You* are not afraid because I pose no threat to you."

"Don't you?" he asked, more curious than assured, as if internally testing the question.

A mad little laugh broke free. "Hardly, Your Grace."

"Ash."

"Pardon?"

"Your Grace will become tedious. Ashbey if you must, but," he hesitated, "I'd prefer Ash."

"Do your other *friends* call you Ash?"

"Yes." Again, he tilted his head. "Though I think of them as allies more than friends."

She tugged on her hand. He held fast.

"Ah, I've misunderstood," he said slowly. "If you weren't, as I now suspect, referring to my *male* friends, the answer is no. And I'd like you to know no other woman has ever joined me in this bed."

"You were married."

"Yes." His gaze shuttered. "She did not...join me here." His tone flattened. "Been reading the peerage, have you?"

Yes. And curious as to why his wife and father had died on the same day. But she had no right to pry. Her throat, suddenly dry, proved remarkably resistant to the apology she wished to offer.

"Ashbey," she managed. "Why am I the first?"

"I haven't any idea." His gaze remained glacial, but its clarity could not be mistaken. He ran a finger along her face. "I respond to a pretty woman, as most men do, but I have felt nothing. Not for a very long time." His eyes warmed. "Until you."

Despite the fire and the silken robe, she shivered. "Until me?"

He nodded. "When I saw you looking at the woman who'd insulted you, I hurt with you. I felt pain."

How could one respond? "And?"

"And I gambled you could make me feel more."

She blushed, hot and full-bodied. And then she stood, even though he still held her hand. Raw fury coursed through her veins.

"My grief is not for sale, Your Grace. Even for an audience of one."

Especially for an audience of one.

PAIN SAILED THROUGH HIM. *Again*. This time, followed by an inner demand.

Do something or she will leave.

In her presence, he became human. Flawed, yes, but real.

"I cannot buy your grief"—he rose to his feet, placing himself between Lady Stone and the door—"any more than I can buy you."

"You can. You have. And you did." She pointed at him in accusation. "And don't you go throwing that free will rubbish in my direction."

He lifted his brows. "You said your chest was tight?"

She frowned but nodded.

"Now mine is, as well." Sensation was glorious. She was glorious. He smiled. "I believe, Lady Stone, that I am frightened you will leave."

"Then why are you smiling?"

"Because feeling is sublime." He rose to his feet and gathered her into his arms.

Feeling may be sublime, but Lady Stone was stiff with righteous fury.

"Is your chest still tight?" he asked.

She blinked, startled. "No."

Bless her, she could not lie.

"Does your heart still pound?" he asked.

Her expression shot daggers. "I will not say."

"You may be angry, but you're no longer scared. Whereas I am full of fear..."

Without taking his eyes from hers, he unlaced his robe and let it fall. She gasped—possibly at his state of naked arousal. He placed her hand against his chest.

"...and desire."

She jerked back as if startled, mouth agape. Then she slowly caressed him with her gaze and wet her lips. *Progress.* He drew her hand to his shoulder and threaded his arm around her waist —a cautious cradle.

"Shh," he whispered. "Shh. Nothing else matters but the heat between us...the magic we will make tonight."

She took a deep breath. Finally, she relaxed, collapsing against his chest with a heartfelt sigh.

He, whom even his allies referred to as Hades, finally held his angel in his arms.

Before this, he'd come together with others—fucked, in common parlance. But this feeling? He would have pledged eternal devotion if she'd demanded he do so.

He *had* pledged eternal devotion. And she hadn't even had to ask. Whatever existed between them, he'd never known its like.

The longing welled deep. His pain—and hers—spun in the ether like woolen thread, thinning and twisting, binding them in knots even he could not untie.

CHAPTER 7

*S*he'd been angry. But her fury, along with his dressing gown, had dropped, disappearing into a pool of desire the way rain blended softly and thoroughly into a bubbling spring.

Either they were swaying, or the room had started to rock. Her weight rested on her right foot, now, her left...but neither foot kept her aloft. Dizzy, Alicia remained upright only because Ashbey held her against his chest as if she were his cherished bride.

She was not his cherished bride.

Nor were they about to indulge in a hasty marital coupling done with discretion beneath the proper shielding of sheets. *Thank heavens.*

He crooned to her, restraining his masculine energy, though its charge hung in the air like a scent, taunting—*tempting*—while his manhood jutted into her belly, already cocked and fully primed.

He'd said something before taking her into his arms. Something that had roused her indignation. Only she couldn't remember his words. She could not remember *any* words, for that matter. Words were stupid and useless, a mere nothing next to the wanton anticipation thrilling her blood.

Tonight, she'd finally understand the sounds that had filled those long-ago evenings. She'd make sense of the shadows she'd seen dancing on the walls. She'd learn passion, unrestrained.

She wanted all the sighs and the other noises of pleasure, and she wanted them now.

Her hands crept up his taut forearms and into the unbelievable softness of his hair. Tentatively, she stroked his neck.

He ceased swaying, and a low rumbling groan tore from his core. The desperate sound unleashed a sense of her power over him. Suddenly, he seemed as if he had been shaped and formed for her and her alone.

"Kiss me again." She lifted her face.

He cupped her chin and guided her mouth to his. His lips slid over hers as he explored her mouth with his tongue. The heat of his mouth promised all she needed. Greedily, she demanded more.

"Slower"—he exhaled raggedly—"I want to savor you."

She shook her head no. Desire's waves were rollicking and fast. Why wade into the ocean when she longed to dive in and submerge?

She hadn't felt him loosen the laces of her dressing gown, but the silk slipped from her shoulders down into the crooks of her arms.

"I want to see you, too." His voice was low and raw. "I want to see all of you. I want you completely bare."

His words unlocked another layer of her reserve. She let the dressing gown fall. Her fine linen shift may have been near-transparent, but a barrier was a barrier nonetheless. She pulled the garment over her head and dropped both her shift and her gaze.

Nothing remained between them. Nothing at all.

Wetness rushed between her legs as she relished his appreciative hum.

"Lovely."

The feminine word from his utterly masculine mouth made her smile.

"You're lovely too," she whispered.

With a chuckle, he hooked an arm beneath her knees and lifted her onto the bed as if she were feather light. The mattress's softness gave way to their bodies and a downy pillow cushioned her head. Never had she felt so indulgent.

"Ah, Lady Stone..."

His tone was a query, but he failed to complete the question. Instead, he occupied his lips with a kiss that began at her ear and then trailed from her neck to her breast.

He was gentle, so gentle. Her earlier fears had been unfounded.

His lips covered her nipple, sending waves of pleasure down her back. He sucked and kneaded and caressed until she broke free of shyness and burned everywhere all at once.

"Impossible," she said with a laugh.

"Impossible, yes," he murmured. "Impossibly soft—"

His rough fingers traced her abdomen, she focused on the friction.

"Impossibly inviting—"

The friction dipped into the cleft between her legs.

"Impossibly," he slipped two fingers inside her body, "tight...and wet."

She held mortification at bay. Mortification belonged to the harsh light of day. She would welcome, instead, the candle-lit darkness and the rhythmic caresses that turned her skin to heat.

Now she understood the pleas that had fallen from the brothel windows.

Yes. Please. More.

She may have even spoken them aloud.

No matter how wide she flowered, his touch asked for something beyond. Asked? No. Demanded. Indirect, her duke was not.

Her duke?

Yes, hers—hers for three nights. She claimed him with a needy groan. Placing her palms against his stubbled cheeks, she grasped his beautiful face and forced his mouth back to her nipple, exactly where he belonged.

"Yes." She twisted. "Please." She sighed. "More." This time, she knew she'd begged aloud. She did not care. Her consciousness coalesced to a single point. *Ashbey.*

His rhythm grew insistent; her body stretched toward his command. She could not parse the sensations that simmered. Craving spooled in her legs, her belly, and her breasts, winding and then tightening until she vibrated with lust from the inside out.

Too much. She flailed and whimpered. She might have even cried.

He didn't listen. He refused her space to breathe. So, she broke into pieces in his arms. Cinders sparked and spun as they rushed through her veins as pure pleasure. Then, slowly, her blood thickened with exhausted satisfaction.

Everything became still, and she was at once both shattered and whole.

Now, Ash knew his lady's passions were intemperate, her desire raw. She'd been uninhibited perfection as her pleasure peaked, awkward and real and trembling to her core. He'd shuddered with her—his retrained desire to her complete release.

Was he numb? Not at all.

Pain sung in his cock—taut, restless pain, demanding release. He did not even try to master his torment. To feel was to be alive. For once, he intended to live.

Sweetness and agony. Satisfaction and surrender.

Beauty personified.

He tuned to her, aware of every movement, no matter how small. His gaze searched her face for some clue as to why *this* woman possessed the key. He found no apparent reason. She remained consummate mystery.

She inhaled and lifted her lids, her wild eyes coming to rest on his.

"Ashbey," she whispered.

He tried not to peacock at the wonder in her voice. He tried, and he failed.

"I'd say the lady has been thoroughly pleasured."

Her lids drooped. She touched a finger to his chest, trailing it softly up his neck to his lips. He tasted his sweat on its tip, and then took her finger fully into his mouth.

"What are you doing?" she asked.

"Providing you with ideas"—he smiled a suggestive smile—"for later."

Her eyes clouded with confusion, then widened as her confusion cleared. She returned his smile with a glint of wicked promise. Giddy gratitude filled his mind.

She stretched, arching her back and spreading her arms. Settling back into the pillows, she subjected him to a thorough visual exam.

He rolled to his side, adjusting his still-stiff member with his hand.

"Do you approve?" he asked.

"Shush," she teased. "I am deciding how I wish to proceed."

"By all means," he stroked his length, "do what you will."

He wasn't sure what he'd expected to unleash with those words, but he did not expect the swift shove that forced him onto his back, rendering him physically vulnerable in ways that might have roused fury if shock had not left him tingling.

Willfully, he stilled his body's power—the same power he'd

wielded against other lovers to restrain, and to ultimately plea-sure. He had never—ever—allowed anyone the upper hand. Yet years of consummate control had earned him no reward.

So, he offered up his body in anticipatory awe.

With a confidence that belied her stated lack of experience, she threw her legs astride his hips. Her weight, a mere nothing, was not what held him in place. His *vision* rendered him immobile.

She was radiant—her skin, lightly coated with a fine sheen of sweat; her nipples, dark pink and pointed. Her lids dipped over sultry eyes, drunk on desire.

She was intoxicated...*with him*. She'd come to him trembling in cold and fear, but now she was in command. Rising onto her knees like an Amazon claiming her prize, she arched over him, took his face into her hands, and teased his lips with a tantalizing kiss.

Again, his muscles demanded he take control. Again, he denied the impulse. Not tonight. Tonight, he would allow his lady to set the pace.

He concentrated on the pressure of her lips. Hers was a perfect mouth. Soft. Inviting. Tasting of sweetness, and promise, and light. Her lips traced a path to his chest. There she paused, pressing her ear against his heart.

A small gesture. Artless and honest and painfully poignant. It was all he could do not to clasp her there.

"What do you hear?" he asked.

"Strength. Steadfast troth."

He did not deserve to possess this angel. If he'd been a better man, he never would have coaxed her to come. If he were a good man now, he would set her free.

"I'm not good."

"I know." She rose onto her knees with a sinful smile. "That is precisely why I came."

He drew her long blonde hair over her shoulder and then

traced the undercurve of her still-swinging breasts. He relished that smile. That knowing, indulgent smile.

How much could a man resist? How much could he possibly take? Evil he may be, but he'd been taken captive by a Dionysian priestess who was ready to perform cultic rites.

"Take me inside you."

Her brow furrowed. "On top? Like this?"

"Definitely like this."

He would die if she did not. Expire. Right there.

His hands climbed up her thighs, guiding her into position. Then, he held his cock at the base, readying himself with an agonizing squeeze.

She lowered herself over his tip, and gasped. Uncertain, with a mild tremor, she looked to him for approval.

He grabbed her delicious ass, and drove up, achingly slow. Inch by inch her body sheathed his member. Wet heat seeped pleasure into his skin. Flashes of heat shot through his sack straight to his toes.

As her soft warmth enveloped him, he could have sworn he'd never been with another woman, the bliss was so unique. And would have sworn to be loyal to her alone.

He wanted only *this* woman.

His fingers branded her soft flesh. If he held tightly enough, perhaps he could defy time. But no, the ancient drive won out.

Take. Her. Now.

He could not deny another internal demand, though he took nothing. She was the one who thieved. He kneaded her breasts, clutched her ass, met every drive with an upward thrust, but she remained in control. She rode him fast—conquering and triumphant; soft, yet hot; powerful yet pliant. She found her rhythm, using it to push him through a messy froth of pleasure, pain, and lust.

Then, she threw back her head and sighed.

Swept up in an irresistible tide, he surrendered. One squeeze of her thighs and he was cast into primordial darkness. The covetous serpent slithered up his legs, wrapping tight around his core. Then, he erupted into her body. In the sudden, blinding explosion, he was fully consumed by heat.

Silence. Darkness. Peace.

Only the feel of her heartbeat guided him back from the deep.

It took far more effort than he expected to lift his head from the bed. But the kiss seemed terribly important, and her sigh was every answer he'd sought.

Nothing this night had gone as planned, yet he fell into a grateful slumber knowing he'd received infinitely more than he had asked.

Forgetting he deserved none of it at all.

CHAPTER 8

*M*orning light filtered through the omnipresent gloom clinging to the castle, coming to rest on the mattress depression that had, last night, cradled the Duke of Ashbey. Alicia stared at the indentation, thinking of the duke's low, rumbling voice, gritty as an ancient fortress—if a fortress could be audible, and could embody the promise of sin. She held at bay anticipatory chills in favor of a healthier scold.

"My lady" is just an expression.

An expression which did not imply affection nor, for goodness' sake, belonging.

Yet, she could not shake the feeling she had become Ashbey's lady sometime during the night. Her lips were tender, and her legs ached in mild protest, as if she'd taken a long and vigorous ride. Secretly, she savored her muscles' resistance. This was what it was to have a body well-pleasured.

She snuggled into the pillow, reliving the salient moments of the extraordinary night. Ashbey, striding into the room, robed like a sumptuous Prince, though shockingly bare beneath. Ashbey, holding her in a tender embrace against his heated skin and swaying as if to music only he could hear. Ashbey, using his clever hands to stroke her intimate places until her nerve endings sung.

It was mortifying to remember the primal force that had then taken control, animating her body so she was compelled to move as she had never moved before. Oh, she'd seen shadows of women and men coming together in strange and thrilling ways. Shadows moving on the walls of the brothel on her tiny island. Shadows that had made her hot with want.

When Octavius was alive, she'd packaged up her secret desires in shame and set them away, determined to be good.

I'm not good.

I know.

She turned her face to her pillow.

A decade of pinned up longing had unraveled in just one night. A frisson of desire ran beneath her skin as she remembered the feel of his hips between her thighs. Back in the dressing room at Marie's, she'd towered over him as he sat. Then, he'd held all the power. Last night, she'd been the one in control.

His lust, his pleasure, his honest, raw need—they had all been for her alone. She could have asked—no, demanded—anything.

She'd called him Ashbey, and not even given him her Christian name. She wasn't sorry. If she'd granted him leave to call her Alicia, she'd have hooked one more stich in a pattern far too dangerous to complete.

She stretched out into the indentation where the duke had slept.

Then again, *had* he slept?

Or had he left after she'd fallen asleep? He'd implied this was his bedchamber but, apart from the rumpled sheets, there was little proof he'd ever inhabited the room.

A strange, hollow feeling threatened from the edge of her consciousness. She knew so very little about the duke. Not that she hadn't searched. The gossip sheets hadn't mentioned his name since she'd been in London, and the Ashbey entry in *The Correct Peerage* listed only names and dates.

More sobering still, he'd visibly prickled when he suspected she'd pried.

She rubbed the base of her palm over her eyes. This exhilaration would not last. The delight must come to an end. She was not a part of the duke's world. She could never be a part of the duke's world.

What would it mean to have been so fully claimed and then to go back? Go back to the endless monotony, the loneness and the pain?

She'd told the duke she'd known pleasure with Octavius. Perhaps that had been what she needed to believe. What she'd called pleasure had been closer to satisfaction, the kind that came after having fulfilled one's duty. But the pleasure she'd experienced last night? That had never happened before.

She scowled.

Correction, again.

What had happened last night had never happened *to her* before.

From what she'd read in the countess's letters, the experience was not uncommon.

She rang the bell, determined to rise.

What was special to her, must be tritely familiar to Ashbey. A man did not display such ease in his skin without extensive experience in the nude. And if she wanted to keep her head...and her heart...she must keep that in mind.

What was new to her was commonplace to him.

WHAT HAD HAPPENED to Ashbey last night had never happened before.

His wild and uninhibited release had filled him with indescribable pleasure and yet, in the moment just before sleep, he'd felt as if he'd given over part of his soul in complete surrender. Last night had been everything he had hoped, but this morning brought home the cost.

Cerberus, his Arabian, sensed his unease and danced. Ash calmed the horse with a soothing stroke to his neck.

Mystical connection was for poets and artists and men who lived for sensation, not for men born to privilege and responsibility, and certainly not for a man hemmed in by a legacy of madness and murder.

Danger lurked in the mere acknowledgement of how deeply he'd been moved. What good would it do? Chev had warned him not to create a scandal for the young widow. And, that wasn't the only reason. He could have no future with Lady Stone.

Lady Stone—he snorted—he did not even know the woman's name.

Ash could not promise Lady Stone a future. He had no future to promise.

Her strange magic had breathed new animation into his veins, but how long could such a feeling possibly last? How long did he have before the darkness converged once again? This strange quickening would pass, and he'd be returned to his numb, void prison.

Lady Stone deserved more. She was far too lovely to imprison as well.

Lovely? She was more than lovely. She had a quality to her, an artless openness in want of nurture and protection. What kind of monster would he be if he forced her to live in his world, knowing what had happened to Liza? To Rachel? To his mother?

If he could, he would have sworn to protect her light. But experience had shown him what would happen if he stayed close. The weighted gloom attached to his world would subsume her light. Gloom as deadly as smoke from an unquenchable fire. The same gloom that had stolen everyone else in his family.

Fog below cloaked the village, the harbor, and the sea. Its fingers even covered the charred portion of Wisterley, vacant since the fire that had claimed both his father and his wife. The single, visible structure was the tower peeking out of the mist. A tower which held Lady Stone.

Ash understood a warning when he saw one.

Chev was right. Lady Stone had suffered enough. For now, Ash could give her pleasure, for a time. She would not wish the alternative.

No one wished to be chained to a man haunted by ghosts.

He urged his horse to a gallop although the rain hit his face in stinging drops.

Two more nights was all he would permit himself to steal. Two nights he intended to savor.

ALICIA SPOTTED Ashbey out the entry hall window. He emerged from fog as if he'd been formed by the storm. The beast he rode looked as ferocious as Satan and was galloping so fast, Ashbey's greatcoat flapped wildly in the wind. All the discomfort and fret building since his absence, all the annoyance she'd cultivated to protect her heart, vanished.

Together, man and beast formed a breathtaking vision. She sighed. He couldn't help that he was striking.

She could never mean to him what he could come to—if she allowed—mean to her. However, to be angry was a fruitless endeavor. Anger at Octavius had been equally absurd.

She meant *something* to the duke. Just like she'd meant *something* to Octavius. Something that made Octavius rescue an orphan from a near-deserted isle and keep her the way one kept an antique doll—a pretty thing to be displayed and never touched.

Octavius had never even carried her over the threshold.

Perhaps Octavius believed her a waif incapable of giving or receiving great passion. If that was so—she smiled—she had certainly proven otherwise.

She shrugged. She had Ashbey. For now. That was all she could ask for. All, in fact, she wanted. Ashbey and his world belonged to some different strata. She had reached too high once before, and intimately understood the consequences.

She turned away from the window and back to her book.

First, he'd stable and brush down his horse, then he would want to wash, then he'd need a bite to eat, and then—

The door clattered open and he strode into the hall, stopping short two long strides past where she sat by the window. His coat arced out as he swiveled.

Intoxicating, those eyes.

She hadn't even realized he'd moved until he took her book from her hands.

"I was reading!"

"Allow me to summarize," he said with mock seriousness. "In the end, she dies. He realizes, too late, the error of his ways."

The corner of her lip turned up. "It's not an unhappy kind of book."

"Evelina?" he read the title.

She nodded. "The heroine was just attacked by drunken sailors and then rescued by prostitutes."

He widened his eyes. "Shocking."

She grinned. "You should try reading it."

He tossed the book onto a table. "I *should* do many things, but what I *choose* to do is take you back to bed."

The flush that darkened her cheeks sent a pleasurable rush through her body. There were many reasons to protest—the sun had not yet set, she had only just dressed, and, and, and...

"Mustn't you eat?" she asked.

"Excellent point." He leaned back and called down the stairs, "Mrs. Kent?"

A muffled acknowledgment sounded from below the stairs.

"A tray in half an hour, please." He raised a wicked brow. "Make that a full hour."

Her grin deepened and he swept her up into his arms.

Octavius had neglected to carry her over a threshold, but Ashbey carried her up two full flights of stairs. Somehow, she preferred the latter.

CHAPTER 9

*E*schewing ceremony, Ash deposited Lady Stone on his bed. The ropes beneath the mattress stretched and then retracted, making her bounce. She laughed, low and throaty, an invigorating sound that oscillated back and forth through his body like a deep caress.

The surge of excitement that followed his all-out gallop merged with the thrill of anticipation.

"When I'm finished"—his smile was predatorial promise—"you won't have the energy to laugh."

"Is that a warning"—she shimmied to the side of the bed and fluttered her lashes over lust-drunk eyes—"or a promise?"

He cupped her face. She was so exquisite. Trusting, too. She had no idea how dangerous he was. If he had his way, she'd be bound to the bed, splayed and twisting with need.

But, he'd vowed not to debase.

He brushed his fingers over her neck and cheeks, memorizing the angles of her face and bathing her in sensation. He stroked the most sensitive places with expert fingers, never dipping his hands below her collar.

Slowly, she surrendered. When her neck relaxed, he moved

his hand beneath her hair, holding her still as he traced her jaw with his lips.

Her whimper was sweet prologue, but he wanted her to ache, to burn. To murmur, as she had last night, an ardent *please* with a look that was only for him.

He nibbled on her earlobe with a hungry, breathy bite, feeling her response. She was trembling. Probably already wet.

He could refrain from subjecting her to physical restraints, but need he deny the potent satisfaction of having her beg for his touch?

No.

He pulled back and stood, folding his hands behind his back. She sat straight, eyes half closed, hands on either side of her thighs, gripping the sheets. She held her lower lip between her teeth—an enticing show of eager innocence that rumbled through his want, loud as thunder.

A crease appeared between her brows. "Would you like me to remove my dress?"

He considered. "Keep it on."

She blinked, looking hurt. "Do you wish me to remain still as well?"

Still? "God, no."

"Then why must I remain clothed?"

He assessed the picture she made—a lady, dressed for a country morn, if with skirts somewhat askew. "You needn't, if that is your wish." He forced a knee between her thighs, and straddled her leg. He made no attempt to hide either his admiration, or his arousal. Her nipples came to delicious points. "However, before you decide, may I show you my wish?"

She nodded.

He loosened her bodice, happy to discover her stays had a little give. He slipped his fingers beneath three layers of fabric and drew out her breasts, one by one, being sure to brush her skin as he tucked away the rumpled bits. At last, she was fully, beautifully exposed.

"Better," he said.

Her cheeks turned a fetching pink. Pink that spilled like punch over her neck and shoulders.

"Are you wet yet?"

She swallowed. "I think so."

He rolled her right nipple between his fingers. "Now?"

"Yes," she whimpered.

He teased the sensitive tips of both her nipples, savoring each hitch in her breath.

She whimpered again. "Please, Ash. *Please.*"

There it was—a rich chord of yearning and supplication. The resonance was flawless. The sound played in him as if he were an instrument, and she, a musician.

His cock shifted beneath his clothes, extending. Her gaze fixed on his tented falls, eyes curious and eager.

"May I?"

"If you wish."

She unbuttoned his breeches. Then, she glanced up. He nodded.

Reaching inside, she cupped his balls with heavenly fingers. She slid her palm down his length. Then, she moved one hand up his member, the other down, until both hands were gliding over his cock. He silenced his own, desperate *please*.

"I'll," he said hoarsely, "never again be able to wear these breeches without getting hard."

She glanced up shyly. "I like touching you."

This was punishment, obviously. Soon, he'd be enfeebled. Prostrate at her feet.

He touched his knuckle to her chin, rubbing his thumb across her lower lip. She parted her lips. Instinctive. Unconscious. Not fully understanding the implied invitation. He halted his thoughts before fully imagining her lips around his cock. If he did, he might spill into her hands—a surprise and a disappointment.

Summoning all his discipline, he caught her wrists in his hands, sunk to his knees between her thighs.

"Lift your skirts."

Curiosity overruled the challenge sparkling in her gaze and she complied.

Now *this*, he decided, was a sight to remember—her breasts, free of the confines of her dress, her shift and her skirts in rumpled confusion, and her white stockings, tied with tight little bows, giving way to peach-colored flesh, and all that invited beyond.

Taking his time, he stroked her folds with his knuckle. Very wet, indeed.

Her mew was lamb-like...hungry and needful. She threaded her hands into his hair. The soft pressure against his neck was all he could take.

Using his lips, he plundered without permission. She gasped, and her knee knocked against his shoulder. She tasted of welcome and warmth. He savored the sensation, then he lost himself to his work.

He found the sensitive nub and teased relentlessly with his tongue.

Her release came fast—too fast. But he did not waste time on complaint. Instead, he hooked his arms beneath her knees, and rose, guiding her onto her back. His cock, rock-ready, needed no assistance. Inch by inch, he slid inside. Her limbs remained limp, and her hazy gaze fixed to the place where they joined until he fully disappeared.

This was bliss—the only true euphoria he'd ever known.

Still standing, he withdrew and then thrust—once, twice. Then, he was overcome. He bowed over her body, feeling her stomach, her breasts, even her small pants of air. He released her legs. She hooked her ankles at the small of his back.

He filled her in wave-like motions while planting light kisses on her cheeks, her lids, her ears, her neck—anywhere, really. His on release amassed, and then his climax ricocheted though his body, touching every nerve—an experience as stimulating as it was exhausting.

He was fully satiated, and still he wanted to beg. What for, he wasn't sure. He only knew that he'd never, ever experienced anything like Lady Stone.

All this sensation when he hadn't even taken off his coat.

She unhooked her legs from his back. Reluctantly, he withdrew. She stretched out across the bed like a wanton, her wrinkled morning dress still shoved up her thighs. He touched the satin ribbon that held up her stocking.

"Very nice." He'd intended to say something more. Something witty and seductive and charming. Nothing penetrated his weary mind. Instead, he ran his nails over her thighs.

She made a sound. A chuckle, perhaps.

"If you can still laugh," he managed a smile, "I must not be finished."

She scooched backwards on the mattress, and made an indifferent attempt to smooth out her skirts. Failing, she folded an arm behind her head.

"Imagine!" She measured her words as if she had just tasted—and enjoyed—some rare fruit she had expected to dislike. "I'd judged fully clothed *coitus* less interesting, but that was surprisingly enjoyable."

He hadn't thought the term coitus could be seductive. Then again, any word that came from her lips would be seductive. Still, he'd have to expand her vocabulary. Not now, but rather when he could think, probably sometime hours into the future.

He'd been right from the start—her hair did look smashing when strewn across his pillow. He'd done terrible damage to the day-dress, but regretted nothing. And from the look in her eyes, neither did she—her eyes were tired but pleasured, bewildered, and slightly amused.

Sweat-teased curls clung to her temples, and crushed and twisted stays lifted her still-exposed bosom. She made no move to cover herself, not that he minded. If she was comfortable with uncovered breasts, he heartily approved. In fact, he'd have Marie make a special dress. One she could wear when they were alone. How interesting it would be to dine across a properly set table, with Lady Stone in full sartorial splendor, absent only the front of her dress.

He moved his legs to accommodate a rush of blood to his groin. Then, he remembered.

Three nights—and one had already passed. Besides that, he hadn't dined at a proper table since the death of his wife, and even those meals had been taken in excruciating silence.

Then again, he hadn't slept in a bed since then, either. Until last night.

Reluctantly looking away, he set himself to rights. Just in time, as well. Mrs. Kent called from beyond the door—a rescue from the uneasy turn of his thoughts. He answered the door, collected the tray he'd requested, then told the housekeeper she could retire for the night.

Now that he had Lady Stone back in bed, he intended to keep her busy—and his mind otherwise occupied.

He set the tray on a bed-side table, removed his coat, and then stretched out by her side, proceeding to feed her, once small slice at a time.

ALICIA REACHED for some of the cheese, Ashbey caught her hand and shook his head *no.*

"Lie back and allow me, love."

"Very well." She nestled into the pillows without readjusting her bodice.

He made an appreciative sound low in his throat. Then, using his fingers, he brought the first morsel to her lips, carefully laying a small square on her tongue. She nipped the tip of his thumb as she savored the salty, tart taste.

His gaze grew warm and intent. "Another?"

She swallowed. "Yes, please."

He fed her piece by piece, with sparing only an occasional bite for himself. The experience was as decadent as the food was delicious. When she'd finished eating, he carefully wiped her lips.

Afterwards, he cupped her neck and rained kisses over her exposed throat. As his lips nipped her flesh, he caressed the length of her body with tenderness, as if she were a hallowed object.

As his lips closed around her nipple, she guided his hand back between her legs. Letting her knees fall to each side, she found her pleasure against the calloused fingers entwined within her own.

She sighed through her final shiver—not just satiated but transported.

Made bold by the growing familiarity of his body, she expanded her own explorations. She touched him in places she'd never dared handle, teaching herself with each flick and stroke and graze how to best elicit Ashbey's deepest, most lustful growls.

And then, she taught herself how to conquer him.

Gently, she templed her fingers around his cock, lowered her head and then wrapped his member with her lips. Strange at first, but not completely unpleasant. His musky, male scent filled her nostrils. He shivered, grunted, and jerked his hips as she moved, loving the sense of intimate connection.

Then, his fingers tangled roughly in her hair. He protested fiercely, but her own fists firmly locked him in place, prevented him from pulling away before he came. She'd dug in her nails feverishly moving her mouth until he released an untamed cry.

She swallowed his bitter taste and lifted her head, wiping her mouth with the back of her hand. She grinned in triumph—her lips, her tongue, and her hands had broken a duke into pieces.

Just a few days past, she would have denied any natural capacity for such inhibition, but with Ashbey, she could be feral without embarrassment—greedy, raw, and grasping.

If Ashbey revealed even a fraction of what they'd done, she would be ruined forever. The thought should have made her feel vulnerable. It did not.

She placed her hand against his stubbled cheek. "Are my secrets safe in your keeping?"

TWICE, Lady Stone had driven him to exhaustion, doing things he would never have asked a lady to do. Devil take him, she'd just swallowed his seed—and that, without hesitancy or shame!

Her exertions had left her flushed. Her lips were red and parted. A light sheen of sweat glistened across her chest. She appeared utterly defenseless and exposed as she asked him softly to take her hidden facets into his care and confidence.

Something tender and protective cleaved his chest.

He gave her his pledge. Unworthy as he was, he would do all he could to keep her safe. "You may trust me. Always."

Her shoulders eased. Her face relaxed. She became again, angelic. But she wasn't an angel. Purity wasn't the quality that lit her from within, but innate kindness. Generosity that even extended into acts of intimacy. How had she survived the shame and heartbreak of her broken marriage with this part of her intact?

There was so much about her he did not know. Accepting her intimate surrender while refusing to delve any deeper struck him as wrong. Unforgiveable, in fact. He ventured a question about her past.

He wanted her trust, too. "Were you happy, at first, in your marriage?"

She looked just as surprised at his question as he was at having asked it. He did not want to know about her marriage. He did not even care.

Except that he did care. Very much.

She replied after hesitation, "In a manner."

"You'll have to explain."

Warily, she gazed into his eyes, weighing something in her mind. He must have passed her test because she began speaking.

"When we first arrived in England, Octavius's father was still alive. He lived in a Rectory with Aunt Hester, and Octavius's brother Simon. That was before Simon joined the Navy. Octavius's father was a rector, you know."

He had not known. Nor did he particularly care.

He wanted to know *her* experience, *her* feelings. He didn't give a damn about anyone else. And, he was envious—resentful, even —of her unceremonious use of the admiral's Christian name. But, he continued to listen, because he'd asked, but also because he would never scorn anything she wished to give.

"Octavius and I were supposed to live with the family, too," she continued. "But Octavius wanted to be close to the sea. So, we rented the third flat above a baker in a small village not too far north of Brighton. I don't know if I was truly happy, but, in that village, at first, I was as content as I've ever been."

He'd take her back to that village if he could—it couldn't be far from where they were. Together, they'd make new memories, washing away the poison her husband had left behind.

Only he wasn't anyone's prize, was he? And he'd poison of his own.

"My window had a view of the remnants of a fortress. I'd read about England when I was young, but I'd never actually seen a castle. You cannot imagine how thrilling it was to be able to see one every morning when I opened my eyes—it didn't even matter that the Castle had been damaged by fire." She chuckled. "I cannot believe I have actually slept in a castle, now."

He masked his surprise. She couldn't be speaking of Wisterley, could she? Certainly, other castles had been destroyed by fire.

But none so close to Brighton.

"What," he wet his lips, "was the castle's name?"

"Oddly enough, no one would tell me. Some sort of superstition, I suppose. Even the vaguest of questions about the family were refused." She shrugged. "We did not reside there long enough for me to earn anyone's confidence. Within a few months, Octavius was called back to sea, and I went to live with his father."

Now, he had no doubt. She'd lived, for a time, in the village little more than a mile from where they were at present. Strange —for once—to be grateful for the same superstitions that had left him haunted and alone.

She sighed. "As my hopes for my marriage faded, the castle view became less and less romantic. The lonely turrets became sad. I wished with all my being that someone would come along and see the beauty there. That someone would rescue the ruin, love the house for all it could be and make it whole once again. Make it a home."

...rescue the ruin...make it whole...

She said the words as if all he needed to do was replace rafters, grind down damaged stone, and simply build again. Nothing connected to Wisterley had ever been so simple.

Her musings lacerated in ways she could never know. For the castle to be whole, *he* would need to be whole.

He held no such illusions.

"Silly, I suppose." She flashed a rueful smile. "But what of you? Were you happy in your marriage?"

The question, though fair, left him even colder than her

description of his castle. He'd asked her the same, however. The same he must answer.

"The idea of happiness had never entered my mind. My marriage was a transaction." Transaction. The perfect word to cover a multitude of sins against Rachel. Against himself.

"A transaction?"

She draped her hand over his. He stared as if his hand was disembodied. What did one do with another's sympathy? He had no idea.

"Then as now, I mixed infrequently with Society. Few would have wed a recluse, fewer still, the son of a man tried for murder."

She made no sound, but he knew the information had come as a shock. He knew because her fingers had briefly lifted from his.

Forsaken, if only for a half second. He hadn't wanted her concern, but its temporary loss was an ache beyond belief.

"Did your father commit murder?"

"The court found him innocent." He'd only acknowledged the truth to Hurtheven. Even Cheverley had never asked. Yet he could not lie to Lady Stone. "But the answer is yes."

She rolled toward him. *Toward* him, not away. She reached up to again cup his cheek. "How awful for you."

He kept his gaze blank. If she saw the riot in his mind, she'd run from the room in horror.

"I was born to privilege," he said. "I have freedoms and honors others do not have. I do not dwell in self-pity." Only in solitude.

And that, to keep others safe.

Internally, he thrashed about within his mind for an alternate question, one what could send Lady Stone out of these treacherous waters. "Do you hate him—the admiral?"

Her thumb had been moving across his cheekbone. Her fingers stilled. She blinked, and then calmly answered, "No."

Astonishing. Rachel had hated him. He'd never begrudged her the emotion. Not until the end.

"Why?" he asked.

"Octavius was honorable," she withdrew her hand.

Even after all the admiral had done, Lady Stone's voice held unmistakable admiration. *She* may not have hated the admiral, but Ash did.

"Honorable and adulterous," he said, "a tricky feat, indeed."

She frowned. "People are rarely one thing or another. The only time Octavius broke his word was when he failed to honor his marriage vows. Whose concern is that but mine? I am not sure, to be completely honest, it was entirely his fault."

"Do you blame yourself for his inconstancy?"

"No," she answered. "But if he were happy, he would not have fallen in love."

He raised his brows. "Have you seen the countess?"

"Of course, I have seen the countess," she said. "I take it you do not read the scandal sheets."

He had, though he'd been searching for descriptions of Lady Stone; nothing else had mattered. But he would have remembered mention of the ensuing scandal, if the admiral's mistress and his wife had met.

"Did you meet accidentally?"

Her bitter laugh chilled. "We did not just *meet*. We three attended the theater, where she occupied his right, and I his left. We arrived together to soirees." Her voice dropped. "She played hostess in my home, before I moved out and she moved in."

Some things, apparently, were too scandalous for even the scandal pages.

His look of horror was genuine. "Terrible."

"For me, yes," she tilted her head, "and for her, too, I think." She held him with a steady gaze. "The countess has great charm and sensibility. She is nearly impossible to dislike."

"Cheverley met her and was unmoved."

She frowned. "Cheverley..." Her frown deepened. "I know that name."

His heart seized, but he nonchalantly folded an arm behind his head. "An old friend from Eton."

"Cheverley..." she repeated.

He could almost see the connections being made. "I doubt you would have met. He served in a diplomatic position during the war, and has been missing for some time."

"Missing? I'm so sorry," she murmured. "A situation no family should bear."

"It's been hardest on his wife. Penelope still holds hope." He lifted his brows. "A love match beyond description from the very start—even I was moved. I helped them elope."

"Really?"

"I rode on the back of the carriage with a pistol in each pocket." He chuckled at the memory. "Chev's father was furious. When he could not annul the marriage, he sent Chev away, hoping he'd never return."

She sighed. "How cruel and unjust."

"Unjust. Yes."

How fetching she was with her brow furrowed and her eyes flashing with indignance. He ran his fingers lightly across her brow, gently smoothing the crease. Her tense expression eased and then she smiled.

How could he be anything but captivated by such radiance?

"Do you truly wish to speak of bygone days?" he asked.

She studied him for a long moment. "Actually, I wish to be in your arms."

Clever woman, Lady Stone.

"Well, then. We are in complete agreement."

He set aside the tangled mess of their pasts, lifted her into his lap, and kissed her deeply, fully embracing their present.

∾

89

ASHBEY HAD FALLEN asleep with one arm angled above his head, as beautiful in slumber as he'd been atop his horse. The sheet covered him to his waist but left bare his muscled torso. Alicia resisted the urge to trace him bicep to tapered waist.

They'd spent their second day alternating between making love and making conversation, so why did he now seem an even greater mystery?

How could someone with an air of such menace be so gentle?

How could a man rarely in society anticipate her every need?

Believing the duke to be a man of power and consummate control had been easy, catching glimpses of the pain he'd repudiated left a cavern in her heart.

Ashbey put her in mind of that castle atop the hill—wounded, sad, and vacant. Like the castle, she wished Ashbey could be healed and made whole. She was certain the force swirling around him like the never-ending storm beyond the window was capable of drawing men to him as easily as it now pushed them away.

If only there were someone willing to bring light back into his life.

She gazed at his slumber-softened features, and tenderness bloomed in her heart. A tenderness that encompassed all she wished for and all she could not have.

The duke could never be hers. And if some small, rebellious part of her heart was wishing the impossible, she had only herself to blame.

She would never be breathtaking like the duke. She would never be dazzling like the countess. She was just Alicia, orphan from the West Indies, childless wife, duty-bound widow.

Even if heaven parted the waters between them, how could she be enough for a man like the duke, when she'd never been enough for Octavius?

The thought caused a stabbing pain. She clutched the cover to her chest.

For the past two days, she'd become someone else. Someone exciting. Someone free. Someone who seized what they wanted. Someone bold.

She was not bold, nor exciting, nor, heaven help her, even free.

She had Octavius's family to care for and protect. And she had to do so in the all-encompassing shadow of the countess and her child.

All she had was one more day. One more day to inhabit this other self. She would do so. And then she would find a way to live in the cold, lonely echo of what had been.

She drew the sheet up to her chin, as if drawing the fabric close could protect her from all she did not know and all she feared she would never understand.

CHAPTER 10

*A*sh never counted the minutes he spent awake at night. Such a task was useless to a man at war with slumber. Eventually, however, in soft, almost imperceptible stages, his bedchamber's darkness lifted, and muted light illuminated Lady Stone. *She* slept the sleep of the innocent—deep and untroubled, her long, even breaths restorative and content.

The contrast to his own restless slumber felt like yet another warning.

Carefully sliding from the bed, he crept toward his retiring room and began his morning ablutions. He peered into his mirror, astonished.

He looked almost human. Almost like an unhaunted man.

She could make a broken man whole, just by standing by his side.

He splashed cold water against his cheeks, trying to shake the sense he'd found something he hadn't known was lost. Danger lurked in such feeling. Tomorrow, she must go.

He finished washing and then glanced to the door. His morning ride was an unbroken tradition. He glanced back to the bed—one more day. There was no contest.

He slid back into bed. She hardly stirred.

Lady Stone.

The hard name did not fit her at all. She was a multi-petaled flower, each layer softer, more delicately fragrant than the one that had come before.

What other parts of her awaited discovery? She'd already overwhelmed every sense he possessed.

They'd had two glorious nights. Nights that had been everything he had hoped for from the moment their eyes had locked.

What a fool her husband had been.

The countess, of course, had left kings tongue-tied. Even queens mimicked her style. But the countess could not have rendered Ash so completely undone. No one could. Only Lady Stone. She had given him back pain and pleasure, fear and anticipation.

Would it be such a terrible thing if he just...kept her?

He could send away the carriage, and lock the doors. He could keep her confined the way he kept himself aloof, and perhaps they could both remain shielded from the gloom.

She'd be his *Persinette*, his lady in the tower. And like the witch who'd imprisoned Persinette, he'd provide her with every luxury. Food, books, musical instruments. Any instruction she'd desire, too.

She could be happy.

She could be his.

Perhaps she'd even escape Rachel's fate.

Perhaps not.

Rachel had been chosen for him by his godfather, plucked from the flowers at Almack's for her pedigree and poise...and for the fact that her family was desperate enough to consider marriage to the heir of a duke once charged with murder.

He'd been dazzled by her beauty. Hopeful with a creature of such refinement by his side, he could restore the family name.

On their wedding night, Rachel had come to him dutifully...and then left in tears, her chest heaving with vitriol. He'd mauled her like an animal, she'd said. She could not stomach his tainted touch. And that hadn't been her worst, or only, accusation.

Another memory intruded, unbidden—Rachel, on the terrace of Wisterley, telling him she hated him as she'd never hated anything before. Telling him he'd ruined her life when he'd brought her to the cursed castle, that she'd rather be dead than married to him.

Less than a fortnight later, she was—along with the father he'd loved and despised in equal measure.

Lady Stone stirred, releasing him from his thoughts. He planted a kiss on her shoulder. Even her skin was sweet.

"Mmmm," she responded.

Carefully, he brushed the hair from her face. "Good morning, Lady Stone."

Dream's mist cleared from her eyes. "Alicia," she whispered. And then, she smiled.

An unfamiliar feeling entered his heart—light and heady, as if he were galloping free.

"Alicia." He tested her name. The consonants spilled over his tongue. *Alicia.*

Now he understood why she had, at first, refused to call him Ash. The gift of her name was more intimate a gesture than anything they'd yet shared.

Too intimate.

He'd pleasured Lady Stone. He could remain thankful, even devoted to Lady Stone from afar. But Alicia? Alicia was someone he must gather up close and protect.

A discordant note clanged in his soul.

The best way he could protect Alicia was to let her go.

"Good morning, Ash."

He gathered her into his arms and held tight.

"Ah, Ash," she sighed.

How could a single sigh transport him from despair to—what

was that word? Was there a word for feeling all would be right with the world?

She pulled away. Her lids swept down as her cheeks pinked. "I require a bit of privacy."

"Of course."

He set her free. Reluctantly.

She glanced back halfway across the room, her shy, sweet, sheepish grin more dangerous than a primed pistol. Then, she disappeared into the adjoining dressing chamber, but not before nervously adjusting her shift.

Why was she nervous? She was utterly perfect. She'd always be utterly perfect. At least, to him. He settled back into the pillows, propping his head on his arm.

The child of a madman, even a madman with a ducal title, was bound to be lonely. His father had never harmed *him*, but he thought it wise to act as everyone else in the household did and keep out of his father's way.

Alone in his chambers, he'd taken comfort in sounds of human activity—cleaning, brushing, polishing...the clank of dishes, the swish of a gardener's scythe. But this was the sound he had longed for—the sound of someone for whom he cared, going about a trivial occupation.

Life, shared.

His chest pierced—the price he'd have to pay for the return of his feeling. But his three stolen days were not over.

She emerged with another, private smile.

Not in the least.

"Will you ride this morning?" she asked.

"Yes."

Her face fell.

"Come here, Alicia." Lud, he liked to say her name. He said it again, "Alicia." He drew her toward the bed. "Alicia." He tumbled her onto the mattress and kissed her until she pleaded for breath.

"I needn't leave the room for the ride I have in mind." With a crude push of his hips, he showed her what he meant.

"You," she said, with a deep-throated giggle, "are a wicked man."

"I want to ride," he said, "and I want—" He stopped.

Dare he reveal what he *really* wanted?

He wanted to bring her to the edge of reason, to show her the outward limit of his sensual imagination—not to debase, but to deepen.

She touched her lips to a spot beneath his jaw. Then, she whispered, "What do you want, Ashbey?"

Lust and invitation filled her voice.

Thus far, their desires had been in accord. No doubt, she'd follow his lead—right into the heart of the cravings he'd vowed to conceal.

"What I want isn't done," he spoke honestly. "Not with fine ladies."

She considered him for a long time. "I am not a fine lady."

He searched her eyes for hesitation, but found only trust. One by one, he drew her hands above her head and then pinned her wrists beneath one of his palms. She was not in the least afraid.

"I want to ravage." His voice cracked.

"Ravage?" She glanced up. "You've already thoroughly plundered."

"You think you've been plundered?" He kissed the tip of her nose. "Not." Her forehead. "Even." Her ear. "Close."

"Would just any woman do for what you have in mind?" she asked, breathless.

His throat dried. "No." This wasn't a game. Not this time. "May I ravage you, Alicia? Will you permit me to give rein to my wickedest desires?"

He traced her beautiful, expressive face, waiting like a coiled snake for her reply.

~

THE SHARP-EDGED PROMISE in Ash's tone left Alicia daunted. Daunted...and excited. The grip he had on her stretched arms hinted at his intent. A fission shuddered through her body—part fear, part uncertain yearning.

"Please, Alicia."

On his lips, her name became a bind that could not be loosened. Not by time. Not by separation. Not by the laws of man.

The gentleness of his finger against her face belied his rough hold and his taut features. If she accepted his sensual demand, he'd reveal the hidden eroticism she'd sensed in him and lead her along the razor thin line where pleasure met pain.

He bowed, resting his brow against her chin. His warm spicy scent filled her lungs, splintering hesitation.

She wanted to absorb all the force he could give, to carry this part of him forever, a memory forged in the light of dawn.

"Plunder and ravage, Ash," she said. "I offer you anything you want."

Some kisses tasted light and sweet, some brimmed with passion and need. *This* kiss was a kiss of fusion, a vow for the present, and a promise of everything to come.

He crushed her body into the pillows, securing her with his weight. Then, he took her nipple into his mouth and swirled his tongue in a slow, aching tease. She sucked in as he rolled the point through his teeth, ending in a soft bite.

Desire stabbed, acute.

He released the bud and the chilled morning air dissipated the pain, leaving a residue of heat. Their gazes locked. His was a wolf's, and his short, swift breath hinted at hunger yet unrevealed.

"Please," she said.

His pupils expanded, darkness devouring light, but he did not yield to her plea. His hands manacled her wrists, thwarting her half-hearted attempts to be free. She arched, forcing an animal sound from his core.

"If you must move, wrap me with your legs."

She hooked her ankles behind his back, resting them on the curve of his ass. His hot skin sizzled against her inner thighs.

"Alicia." He slid his hand beneath her hips. "Alicia."

His chest blocked her view, but she didn't need sight to know she was poised for him to enter. She shivered as his member's tip brushed against her intimate folds.

"Alicia." He inhaled. "I like the feel of your name." His cock teased her entry. "I like the sound of other words, too. Common words. Forbidden words."

"Oh?" she rasped.

The corner of his mouth turned up. "Let's make a beast with two backs, shall we?"

She didn't have to answer. His thrust rendered her utterly full. They blended together in a way she could almost taste—sugar and lemon, wet, tart, sweet. Then, he pummeled.

Ashbey. Ashbey. Ashbey. Each gasp sounded his name.

A tell-tale quiver began in her legs. But before that aching pleasure could spread relief through her veins, he withdrew.

"No!" She nipped his shoulder.

"Patience." He nipped her right back. "You'll get your due in time."

She barely noticed he'd released her wrists. Her eyes stung, but her body wept with craving.

Wrapping her in his arms, he lifted. She clung to his shoulders as he pinned her body against the wall. One leg dangled, not quite reaching the floor. His muscle held her in place and his driving thrusts resumed. The only softness she could find slid through her fingers as she clutched his hair.

Glimmers of release shimmered behind her lids. But again, just before the spark exploded, he withdrew.

"Ashbey, *please.*"

"Soon," he whispered.

Soon? Involuntary quivers had stolen her strength. She had nothing left to give.

He carried her back to the bed like a child. Gently, he lowered her down.

"Stay, until I say."

Cool air swirled around her body, raising tiny, tingling bumps beneath her skin. He, too, remained still—a naked man in full arousal, without any sense of haste.

He'd been wrong. Restraint—not power—was the ultimate aphrodisiac.

Ashbey was neither at the mercy of his cock, nor her need. He was a pause in a symphony, the calm center of a raging storm. But the hardness in his cheek and the fire in his eyes exposed latent brawn.

For that look, for that ever-so slight smile, she would yield.

"Kneel."

His command flushed her cheeks; she came slowly to her knees.

"Now, lace your hands. Like this."

He angled her body away, and arranged her hands behind her head.

"Good."

Fear rippled through her stomach—to be blind to his body was to be blind to his intent.

Could she trust?

The bed dipped behind her, she resisted the overwhelming urge to turn.

He gathered her hair and draped it over her shoulder. He touched his lips—and only his lips—to a spot on the back of her neck just beneath her hands. Fire charred his mark, and then burned a trail down her spine before flaring between her legs.

He placed a comforting hand against her hip. "Alicia."

She closed her eyes. "Ash."

His arms encircled her body, and then he teased her breasts, coming close to, but never quite reaching, the sensitive points. Every heavenly caress left her deeper in want. She longed for him to touch her nipples, to roll them between his fingers, to bite them again. But he just continued to knead, making her wait.

"I can't," she whimpered. "I just cannot."

"Cannot what?" He sounded amused.

"Curse you, Ashbey. You know what I want. Touch me!"

"Where?"

Shame warred with curious need. He would not force her to say, would he?

He withdrew both his hands. She almost collapsed.

Strangely, she knew he would not deny her if she turned and forced him onto his back. But neither would he offer this part of himself again. She wanted Ash. All of Ash. Especially the parts he'd kept hidden.

"My nipple," she whispered. "Touch me there."

He drew her back against his chest. Solace, sweet solace, to feel his warmth. He rolled her nipples through his fingers, grinding his cock against her ass. Visceral tautness stretched between her breasts and that spot between her legs.

"Do you still want?" he asked.

She nodded.

"What do you want?"

"I want your," she hesitated. "Your—"

"What, love?" Breath grazed her ear. "So many words you could choose." He nipped her earlobe. "Dagger. Augur. Jock."

New wetness seeped between her legs.

His lips dropped to her neck. "Brush. Pleasure-pivot. Pump handle..."

She chose the one she'd heard on the docks. "Cock. I want your cock."

His member twitched against her ass. "Lewd woman." He traced her spine before guiding her down to her hands. With a nudge of his knee, he widened the space between her thighs. "A lewd woman with a pretty vulva."

Another full-body tremble. The reasons men kept a woman's vocabulary limited suddenly made sense. She was sure to be hot and ready every time she thought of his voice, of the words he'd just used.

He ran a finger over her wetness. "Do you prefer Grove of Venus? Alas, no shiver. Shady Spring? Apparently, not. Quim? Yes, that's better..." He lowered his voice. "Where should I put my cock, Alicia?"

She inhaled through her parted lips. Cock had been hard enough to say. She simply couldn't bring herself to describe her own intimate body parts.

"I want you inside me."

"Good enough."

She fought the urge to buckle as all his ferocity unleashed. She didn't care. She wanted nothing more than another thrust, to be caught up in a swirling storm of pleasure. He gave her that and more.

He gasped out words, punctuated by the slap of their thighs. She only dimly comprehended their meaning, though they left her panting and shoving back for more. Then, his hard stomach touched her spine, and he threaded his fingers through hers.

He shifted their weight on a single arm and forced her hand to her breast, and then further down.

"Make yourself come."

She may have blushed, she couldn't tell. She was past mortification and shame. She stroked with feathery touches, brushing him, too, where they joined. She was lifted like a leaf in wind, tumbling through forces she couldn't see. Tiny sparks touched the inner corners of her eyes. She moaned and bowed her head, shaking in his arms.

He wrapped her hand around his tightened sack. His breath changed, and then he roared.

Even if there had been someone to hear, she wouldn't have cared. This was a raid, a claiming. There was no place for prudence.

His seed spilled warm into her body, and, in the end, they both collapsed.

She rolled onto his chest, still trembling. His forearms flexed as he held her close. Even weakened, his embrace contained all.

A special kind of awe stole her words. She had been Alicia, orphaned waif, spurned wife, and lonely widow. Now she was Alicia, worshiped, revered and ravaged.

She lifted her face.

He did not look as she expected to look—conquering, triumphant, the mirror of his predatorial smile. Instead, he held his breath, watching her with wary, guarded eyes.

He anticipated censure.

Instinctively, she knew he would not believe if she told him she felt cherished, and, in a strange way, freed. She needn't hold herself to impossible expectations of purity and reserve.

"Ash?" she asked.

"Yes?" he answered.

"I'm hungry."

For a long moment, he just stared. Then, he started to laugh. How she loved the sound.

"Well? Are you going to feed me?"

He kissed her brow, and then went to don his banyan. In response to her quizzical look, he explained, "Mrs. Kent won't be awake for another hour. I will see what I can find."

What kind of duke protected his servant's sleep?

Ashbey wasn't just any kind of duke. He was...

He was...

Oh *no*.

Ashbey was a duke she could love.

He returned with a plate of dried meat and cheese. He handed her his find. She handed it back.

"Feed me."

"Minx," he said to her lips.

He placed a tasty morsel on her tongue. And then another. They sipped wine from a single cup. The heady sensation added to Alicia's dream-like state. He dribbled the last drops of liquid over her stomach, and then followed the trail with his mouth.

Later, she returned the favor.

Throughout the day's remainder, they alternated between food and amorous congress.

He introduced her, gently, to new things—binds that constricted her body, but set loose her most sensual side. He trussed her with a crumpled cravat, her stockings, and even the ties that held back the drapes on the bed. He unlocked her passions, and she held him in complete trust.

When at last the night was dark and they lay exhausted and still, they laughed like children who'd played a naughty prank. She rested her aching body in his arms, and fell into slumber with the pressure of his lips against her hair.

CHAPTER 11

*A*licia awoke to an empty room. Her travel clothes hung from a hook on the wall, just above her packed valise—both signs that Mrs. Kent had been inside. But the only sign of Ash was the scent permeating the rumpled sheets and the dull ache between Alicia's thighs.

She listened for sounds from the connecting washroom—silence.

Fear upended her heart.

She scrambled to her feet, dashed into the dressing room—empty, but for his banyan.

She shook her head no. Ash would not have *left*. Not without saying a proper farewell. He was just out for a ride.

Please let him be out for a ride.

She went to the window. Heavy mist hung in the air, obscuring her sight, though branches emerged from the grayish foam as if floating, unattached. The effect was disturbingly grim.

Even if Ash was out there, she wouldn't be able to see him.

Her fear turned to dread, threatening to spread outward from her heart in permanent cracks. For three days, Ash had pleasured her, fed her, held her, and in turn, she'd relinquished her only true possession—her body. She'd trusted him, opened to him, granted him every desire. Even if he were a devil duke as he claimed, he would not abandon her on the morning they were to part.

He owed her a proper goodbye. One that would acknowledge her consummate surrender, one she could hold close through the lonely nights to come.

She searched back through the prior night, seeking for something she might have done wrong. She found none. She'd betrayed her hope for a different end into the silence of her heart, but never aloud.

There was no way he could have known she was falling in love.

She held her hands to her cheeks. Calm. She needed calm.

And she needed to get dressed.

The simple tradeswoman's dress in which she'd arrived wasn't made for women with time and help to spare, but her shaking fingers made fastening the ties almost impossible.

She prayed Ash would be waiting for her below, but deep inside, she knew the truth. When she descended into the empty hall, she felt no shock.

"Miss, is that you?" Mrs. Kent called up from the kitchens below.

"Yes." Her voice wobbled, teetering on despair.

She'd thought she'd touched Ash's heart as deeply as he'd touched her own. She'd been wrong. So very wrong.

What kind of person bought a woman's body, coaxed her to give him her soul, and then disappeared, without the smallest gesture?

She hadn't expected gratitude. Kindness would have been enough.

Mrs. Kent came up the stairs.

"He's gone, isn't he?" she asked.

Mrs. Kent's gaze flicked to the door, and then she dropped her eyes. But Alicia had already seen the flash of disapproval.

"I've made cakes for your travels."

"Thank you." Alicia couldn't force a bite if she tried.

The door opened. Alicia's heart stuttered as she turned.

"The carriage is ready, ma'am." Mr. Kent bowed, looking weary.

"Thank you," she forced again.

How could he not be here?

Nights, she reminded herself. They'd agreed to nights. Not to mornings. Not to sentimental goodbyes.

How could he not be here?

She lifted her chin. This wasn't the first time she'd suffered humiliation. She would get through this, just like she got through Octavius's rejection, his affair, and his death. Just because Octavius had never made her feel precious—

Her shoulders heaved.

"Oh—Oh, dear." Mrs. Kent rushed up the remaining stairs and enveloped Alicia in an embrace.

"Moll." Mr. Kent's tone reprimanded.

"'Tis not my place," Mrs. Kent said with a stony glare. "But this isn't right. None of this is right. Never thought he'd be as callous as his—"

"*Moll.*"

Mrs. Kent harrumphed. "'Tis the devil's own work to let her go without a by-your-leave. And here I thought she'd be the one."

The one?

Mr. Kent's troubled gaze came to rest on Alicia. "Pay her no mind. The carriage is prepared."

Alicia nodded, gathering her wits. She may feel as if she'd shattered, but she was whole. Whole, if with a breaking heart.

She squeezed Mrs. Kent, grateful for the sympathy, but Mr. Kent was right. Whatever despair she may feel, Ash—no, she would think of the Duke of Ashbey as *his grace* or *the duke* from now on—had not lied. *His grace* had acted precisely how he had warned her he would act.

Truth was a harsh salve.

"I am ready," she said.

Mr. Kent nodded. "I'll retrieve your bag."

"Oh!" Mrs. Kent said suddenly. "This came for you this morning." She rushed to the sideboard and returned to deliver a package.

Alicia unwrapped the brown paper. A cloak—she shook out the fabric—but a cloak like none she'd ever seen. The outer layer was black wool, and the inner lined with the thickest, blackest fur she'd ever seen. Her mind went blank; all she could do was blink.

...a coat of sable.

Mrs. Kent looked away. "His Grace ordered it the night you came. Mr. Kent rode all the way to Brighton."

She touched the lining—rich and smooth and supple. A coat like this could keep her in constant coal for a year or more. A coat like this would remind her of the dark, sumptuous nights they shared.

"Do you have the cloak I was wearing when I came?"

Mrs. Kent shook her head no. "Destroyed on His Grace's order."

She pursed her lips. She didn't want this. She didn't want something that would remind her of this awful moment. But she'd freeze without the protection of a coat.

"Take it, please."

Mrs. Kent did not. Alicia laid it gently over the rail and made her way back up the stairs through his bedchamber into the dressing room. She spotted his banyan on the wall, grabbed it from the hook, held the cloth to her face and inhaled.

Her body, not truly understanding the morning's change, instantly relaxed.

He was a devil—a devil for whom she cared so much more than she wished to care. And if he wanted her to have a memento, she much preferred this. She rolled up the banyan and tucked the bundle under her arm.

With her head once again held high, she returned below stairs to say her goodbyes.

She wasn't certain what point she'd proven, if she'd proven one at all. But at least she could look forward to four more hours wrapped in his scent.

She stepped onto the stair the coachman had positioned to help her into the coach. A lump the size of a pumpkin lodged in her throat.

Stay. Stay and fight.

She closed her eyes to squeeze out the threatening moisture. He'd made his wishes clear.

She would heal. She always healed. And if she ever permitted herself to look back, she would do so only to wonder if it had happened at all.

She would leave his grace behind.

ASH SAT ATOP CERBERUS, looking down at the tower.

Leaving Alicia had been the hardest thing he'd ever done. He'd had to summon a wall of pure will to counter the onslaught of sentiments he did not even know how to define. Vicious, jagged emotions that sliced though his being like shards of broken glass.

When he'd left, he'd planned to gallop fast.

Fast enough for the wind to lash his cheeks. Fast enough to drown out the protestations ringing incessantly in his ears. Fast enough to leave the demons behind.

The weather had not complied.

A tortoise could have passed him at the pace he'd picked his way up the hill—the mist reluctantly unveiling no more than a yard of the path at a time. Now, at the summit, the fickle fog parted just enough to reveal the tower.

He groaned.

The whole morning had the marks of torture, as if he'd been leveled with yet another celestial curse. He'd been cursed before, of course, but this was a stronger damnation, a curse for a devil who'd dared steal one of heaven's own.

He blinked down at the tower, fighting a sting in his eyes.

He had no choice but to leave, he argued with himself for the thousandth time. Repetition did nothing to ease his roiling gut. Even his dark beast danced, imploring him to remedy his wrong.

"If I had asked her to stay, we both know what would've followed."

He conjured—on purpose for once—the memory of his dead wife. He wanted the pain of Rachel's censure—a reminder of the damage he'd done. All that came was the image of a bare Alicia, trussed with his black silk cravat, bliss shining on her face.

One night with him had been too much for Rachel. Three nights with Alicia had only whetted his taste and deepened her appetite. She *had* followed wherever he'd led. And now, he'd left her alone.

Every fiber of his being screamed to drive Cerberus down the hill. Enter the hall and then fall to his knees and beg her to stay. His unspoken supplications burned like acid on his tongue. He gritted his teeth.

Yes, he craved her light. But what had he to offer in return?

Darkness and perversion. A history of scandal and madness and death.

"She would be smothered," he said aloud. "Dead, even if she managed to survive."

Cerberus threw his head and snorted.

Ash scowled. "What do you know? You're a horse."

And then, as if seeing the tower had not been torture enough, more of the mist dissipated. At the center of the picture, an empty carriage.

He'd never intended to watch her go. But now... Perhaps, a

glimpse.

Please.

Just one, last glimpse.

He held his breath to suppress the sensation of her head resting against his chest. Then Alicia—his unattainable angel—emerged.

She walked with the regal posture of a queen—a doomed queen. He'd known at least she'd be warm, but she was not wearing the sable.

The little fool wasn't wearing any cloak at all.

She would freeze.

Damnation, she would freeze.

Cerberus snorted and stamped.

She looked over her shoulder, as if heeding something from the hall beyond. Mrs. Kent came out, retrieved a bundle from under Alicia's arm, and shook out...

He frowned. What the devil was she doing with his banyan?

Mrs. Kent held the garment as Alicia put her arms into the sleeves. Even from this distance she looked ridiculous, like a child in the court robes of a king.

And so lovely he wanted to weep.

If she turned, she would see him. If she turned, perhaps, she would come to understand. She paused with one foot on the step provided by the coachman.

Please. He prayed.

She lifted herself into the carriage and firmly closed the door.

Heaven did not hear prayers from hell.

Loss spread out like a poison vine in every muscle. He leaned forward and hung his head. She'd taken his banyan—the one Cheverley had sent him from the Far East. But he couldn't rouse himself to anger. She could take anything he owned, and he would not protest.

The carriage rattling down the drive carried the last thing that mattered to him—his heart.

CHAPTER 12

*A*licia stared out the rear window of her parlor, her gaze fixed on a blackthorn bush. She hadn't known how to identify the bush whose black branches made a striking contrast against the courtyard's red brick wall, not until she'd encountered a whole hedgerow of them the night she'd gone to meet his grace.

Throughout the month of February, she felt a kinship to the blackthorn's twisted branches. She, too, had been prickly and dark, twisted and bare. But the month had turned, and the blackthorn branches had filled with pink buds, heralding the onset of spring.

In old Irish tales, heroes who were being chased could throw a blackthorn branch, and an impenetrable hedge of thick wood would emerge from the ground, saving them from destruction.

She, too, she decided, could be saved. Even without fairy-story magic, the world was wide enough. Refuge could be found. Somewhere. Somehow.

"Alicia!" Aunt Hester's sharp tone cut through the haze of her reverie.

She hadn't been listening. Again.

In defense, she'd grown tired of the same conversation. Would Simon, when he arrived, be able to sort out the will? Would the Admiralty truly allow the countess to take everything that should be theirs? Outrage had deadened Hester to any other feeling. Octavius's aunt now survived on stalwart moral superiority alone.

Moral superiority Alicia did not share.

"Pardon," Alicia said, "I missed the question."

"I was speaking of the doctor."

"The doctor?"

"The doctor who is to visit this afternoon," Hester said with some exasperation.

As if on cue, the bell rang.

Clearly, she'd missed more than just a bit of repetitive complaining. She listened for the butler's sound in the entry beyond.

"Dr. Wilton," the servant announced.

Alicia recognized the name from The *Herald*. Dr. Wilton was the Royal family's physician. Even with the most drastic economies, his fees would far exceed their ability to pay.

The doctor entered the rear parlor and introductions were made.

"I am afraid there has been some mistake," Alicia said.

"Are you not the widow of Admiral Stone?" he asked.

"Yes, but we did not—"

The doctor cleared his throat. "I believe my message was clear."

Alicia opened and then closed her mouth. "...If you would be so kind as to remind me?"

"I am here to see to the health of the family." The doctor looked from woman to woman. "My fees have already been paid."

"Paid?" Alicia frowned. "By whom?"

"Someone grateful for Admiral Stone's service, no doubt,"

Hester said. "Perhaps it was your father's distant cousin, the one you went to visit last month."

Alicia's stomach somersaulted. And then somersaulted another time. A bitter taste nudged up her throat.

"If you will excuse me." She rushed though the dining room, down the back stairs, and out the door to the garden.

The world around her swerved as she heaved. Nothing came, of course. She hadn't been able to fill her stomach all day. Slowly, she stood. The bud-filled branches of the blackthorn bush swayed in a breeze, adding to her sense the earth had moved.

With shaky legs, she sat. Not good.

None of this was good. If someone impressed by Octavius's service had wanted to help his family, why hadn't they done so before? And the non-existent cousin was certainly not the source. That left the Admiralty. And why would they be concerned with the family's health?

She placed her hand over her belly.

A terrible suspicion had been nudging her since the second week of her sickness. If true, what would happen then?

She turned her face to the heavens and inhaled. Perhaps the sickness was just nerves. The alternative was too horrible to contemplate.

She made her way back into the house as Hester was entering the hall.

"There you are," she said. "Dr. Wilton would like to speak with you now."

Her? "Certainly."

She entered the front parlor and closed the door. The doctor's eyes fixed to her still-shaking hands with interest.

"Dr. Wilton," she said. "I must know the source of the charity bestowed on us."

The doctor lifted his brows. "I could not tell you if I wished, because I do not know. A solicitor requested that I visit you and paid my usual fee."

She sunk into a chair. "But why?"

"That is a question I *can* answer," the doctor said. "He mentioned an unusually high laudanum bill."

She exhaled. "Aunt Hester."

Dr. Wilton nodded. "I have surmised as much. And I've cautioned her against increasing her dosage."

Who knew about the laudanum? The apothecary, of course. No one else. Although... Hadn't the duke paid the apothecary the same night he'd paid Marie?

She frowned. A pernicious turn of thoughts. She did not number in the duke's concerns. He had made his position clear on that final morning. And she hadn't heard a word since.

"You look a bit peaked, my lady."

She folded her hands in her lap. "Just strain."

"Might you permit an examination?"

She eyed him with suspicion. "Would your recommendations be given in the strictest confidence?"

His brows rose. "Of course."

The brief examination consisted, among other indignities, of allowing the doctor to listen to her heart and answering his questions. When he was finished, he sat back down and drummed his fingers against the table, his expression troubled. She imagined he was counting months. Then, he said the words she'd been dreading to hear.

"Lady Stone, is there any possible way you could be with child?"

Aunt Hester's shocked gasp came from the doorway. "Alicia, is it true?"

The room tilted yet again.

She couldn't be with child. Any child she bore within a year of Octavius's death would be considered his whether she protested or not. A miraculous heir was certainly not a part of the Admiralty's plan.

As for the child's real father? She'd promised him three nights.

A bastard had never been part of the bargain.

EVER SINCE THE doctor's visit, Hester had been like a woman possessed. No amount of pleading or reason had shaken her off course. She was convinced that Alicia had somehow contrived to see Octavius on his last leave, impossible though even that timing could be.

As far as Hester was concerned, this child was an answer to her prayers—a legitimate heir.

Alicia should have known Hester would contact Captain Smith. And now that he'd come to call, what had been her private problem was now a matter for the Admiralty.

"A pregnancy changes everything," Hester continued in an excited fever. "It was one thing to consider the codicil while the duchess claimed to have the admiral's only child, it is quite another if the admiral has a legitimate heir."

Alicia felt the captain's eyes, but refused to look in his direction.

"You are correct," Captain Smith said. "The Admiralty will have to take into consideration an heir." He paused. "Correct me if I'm wrong, but didn't the admiral join the fleet a month before he died?"

"Yes," Alicia whispered.

"And it's been two since his death?"

Alicia nodded.

Aunt Hester lifted her chin. "Any child born of a man's wife is considered by law to be his own. Indeed, the law allows a year after the father's passing for a widow to give birth."

Alicia had heard these arguments daily.

As far as Hester and the world were concerned, this child would be a Stone. Alicia wished she could agree. It would be the easiest choice. Little for her would change, but for the addition of a child.

But then she thought of Simon and of Octavia—Octavius's true heirs.

What was she to do?

Ashbey. She squeezed her eyes closed. She could imagine only cold dismissal from a man who hadn't even given her the dignity of a goodbye.

She wanted this child. She wanted this child so badly she could smell its baby-new skin, feel it's tiny fingers wrapped around her thumb. Only, what kind of life could she offer?

Her child's choices would be a lifetime of lies or a lifetime of shame.

"Aunt Hester," Alicia barely recognized voice, "I wish to speak with the captain alone."

"Lady Stone, you know that would be—"

"Absolutely within the bounds of reason," Alicia interrupted, "given my condition and the captain's connection to the Admiralty."

"I see no harm," the captain said.

"Aunt Hester," Alicia raised her brows, "if you would just wait in the hall."

Hester huffed. "Of course, but I will leave the door ajar."

Alicia went to the window, hoping the sounds of the street beyond would muffle sound. She waited for a carriage to clatter by before she spoke.

"Would a child born this winter be considered heir to Admiral Stone?"

The Captain's expression was unreadable. "It is possible, yes."

She pressed a fist to her lips.

"What will you do?" he asked.

"I don't know." She turned away from the window, searching the Captain's face for something familiar, some small thread that tied him to her past. She was more certain than ever that she'd known him once.

Her father had died just weeks before the arrival of *The Maitland*. She remembered her grief, her distress. In a place where lives were short and harsh, her father had done little to protect her beyond leaving a modest amount in the funds. Even a small sum caused the men of the island to circle like vultures...

Then came Octavius, and his ship full of gallant officers.

She frowned, looking past the leathery texture of the Captain's face, conjuring the face of the boy he'd been. *Cheverley.* She'd known she recognized the name the duke had spoken.

"Lady Stone, if you will permit me to suggest—"

"Haven't you done enough, *captain*?"

He looked stricken. "You have me at a loss, Lady Stone."

"I *knew* I could not recall an officer named Smith." She took a deep breath. "Cheverley, correct?"

He blinked. "My lady, you are clearly overwrought—"

"Is it a coincidence, Lord Cheverley, that you are connected to the Duke of Ashbey?"

The captain's gaze sharpened. "Ashbey?"

She had been so, so foolish. "*His grace* knew enough about Octavius's debts to place me in his. How?"

Lord Cheverley's expression was proof enough of his guilt. She pressed her hands to her head and began to pace.

"I prayed and prayed and prayed for a child and none was given to me. When my husband found another, I suffered in silence. Then *he* found me. And now, the life of an innocent will be forever bound to a devil because you gave him the ammuni—"

"Lady Stone!"

She froze, breathing heavily. "Forgive me. The fault is mine alone."

"Not yours alone," he said quietly.

No. Not quite. One devil duke was intimately involved.

"I—I trusted a friend..." His voice faded.

"A friend?" She snorted. "Can a recluse have friends?"

A strange fire glowed behind his eyes. "The man I knew would never have taken advantage of your grief. I wish I could make this up to you. I just..." He paused. "I cannot tell you how sorry I am."

His remorse was real. So was the deep well of concern behind his eyes.

Good God. For the first time since the doctor had spoken, the truth penetrated her heart. She was going to have a child. Not just a child, but *Ashbey's* child.

"This is none of your concern," she said.

"Is there anything I can do—anything at all?"

"You can keep my secret."

"Ah," he sighed. "Even you will not be able to keep your secret for long."

She slanted him a look.

"Unless you marry," he continued, "or bare the child in secret and send him or her away, the child will be considered the admiral's heir."

She kneaded her aching brow. She thought of the print she'd seen the day of the funeral. Of the little girl with her hands pressed in prayer.

"Octavia is Octavius's heir." Octavius's only heir. The child he'd claimed.

"*Simon* is the admiral's heir," the captain replied. "Unless you bear a child."

She frowned. "The Admiralty has decided the codicil is not valid then?"

The captain's expression gave nothing away.

"But surely," she insisted, "the Admiralty intends to honor Octavius's wish and see to Octavia's care."

He looked out the window, crushing his hat in his left hand. "That will be up to Simon."

"Octavia deserves the protection of her father's family."

"In this, I heartily agree. But I am not the Admiralty." His icy gaze returned to her and he lowered his voice. "What of your child, Lady Stone? Does not your child have just as much right to Ashbey's care?"

She placed her arms around her waist.

In her mind, she saw that coat. That outrageously expensive coat. The duke had used debt to lure her in, luxury to cast her off.

A man like that could sire a child, but he would never be a father.

"The duke has made his wishes clear."

"Does he know?"

"No," she finally admitted.

"Are you certain he would fail to provide for the child if he did know?"

She was sure of nothing where the duke was concerned.

He could allow the child to be recognized as a Stone. He could shrug and tell her to live by her wits. Or, he could do the thing she feared most. He could rob her of her child.

Cheverley spoke again, "Lady Stone, you must let him know."

There was censure in his tone. But he hadn't been there. He hadn't wept through a long, cold ride home, hoping every horse that passed carried Ashbey, who'd come to tell her he'd changed his mind.

She hadn't been as wretched since the night her father had died, and she lost the last soul on earth who cared if she survived.

"Must I?" She placed her hand over her stomach and vowed her child would never feel the like. "The duke did not want me, and he most certainly will not want this child."

CHAPTER 13

*T*hunder roiled, drifting like a malignant spirit over the London night, heightening Ash's desolation. He'd thought absence of feeling was his lowest possible point, but this incessant torment was worse—a twenty-four-hour struggle against the basest part of his soul.

Daily, his wicked desires threatened to seize control. He dreamed of breaking into Alicia's home, carrying her off to his castle, and confining her to his bed. He countered his thoughts with the phantom scent of charred flesh.

And everyone had thought *his father* mad.

He prepared for another night of wrestling without a hint of relief in sight. Then, his study door crashed open. *Chev.*

"Christ, Ash! I never thought *you* would play the villain—you who have suffered so much at the hands of others." A shocking amount of venom laced Cheverley's words. "How could you?"

Ash squinted. "What the devil are you talking about?"

Chev stalked into the room. "How dare you trouble Lady Stone?"

Cheverley had somehow discovered his secret. The doctor, perhaps? Dr. Wilton had sworn to be discreet.

"Don't you have anything to say for yourself?" Cheverley asked.

All that self-righteous fury. For what? Because he'd dared to touch something pure? Poison rose in Ash's blood.

"The widow and I had an arrangement. It is not uncommon."

An ugly rage twisted Cheverley's features. "Damn you."

Ash's gaze narrowed. "If you wished to protect your pure little friend, why dangle her like a lure?"

"I thought you were a decent man," Chev answered. "I came to you because I *thought* this was the one place I needn't worry about the spread of scandal."

"You came to me," Ash said bitterly, "because you did not wish to return home."

Chev shook his head no. "I've been your friend. For years. I *trusted* you."

Ash stood. "...And doesn't that just make you feel noble? The always reliable Chev. Friend to the friendless, the first boy at Eton with courage enough to champion a murderer's son."

"I have fought by your side."

"And I have stood by yours while you made vows to a woman who is still waiting for you, not knowing are alive. What are you doing here, Cheverley? Why not go home?"

Chev's gaze narrowed. "This is not about Pen!"

"Isn't it?" Ash asked.

"You have *no idea* what I did to survive for Pen and Thaddeus. For Hurtheven. For *you*."

The wild fire in Chev's gaze couldn't be faked. Still, Ash pressed on. "Why meddle in the affairs of a widow while your own wife pines? It's cruel."

"You know cruel, don't you?" Chev shoved Ash's chest. "I owed it to the admiral to sort out his affairs, and I was close to a resolution. Then you interfered. You have destroyed her chance for peace."

"Her ruin is your fault, you know," Ash taunted. "You

described an angel. How could a devil like me resist stealing a feather from her wings?"

Chev's left hook hit him with shocking force, leaving him teetering on his feet. Ah, the sweet relief of physical pain.

"She deserved protection." Chev landed another punch. "She deserved freedom." And another again. "She did not deserve *you*."

Ash knew that. God, how he well he knew. "Pity. I defiled her just the same."

Cheverley lunged with a full-body roar, knocking them both to the ground. The puckered scar at the end of Chev's arm passed over Ash's eyes.

"Hit me back, you cur," Cheverley demanded.

The lights around Ash flickered. "No."

"Do you want me to murder you? Do you wish to die?" Chev's face blurred. "Because I've seen death. I've looked it right in the eye, and it's not to be wished."

Ash had seen death, too. His father's valet, impaled on his father's sword. The unrecognizable bodies of his father and his wife.

"Perhaps," Ash tasted blood on his tongue, "I no longer have a reason to live."

Chev stared for a long, silent moment. His pallor slowly returned.

"Go ahead," Ash taunted. "Exact your revenge."

"Oh, be silent, would you?" A ragged breath shook Chev's body. His accusatory gaze sliced with a boning knife's precision. Then, he closed his eyes. "Forgive me, Lady Stone." He moved aside. "You have an excellent reason to live, you self-indulgent, addle-pated ass."

Ash's snort caused considerable pain at the bridge of his nose. He lifted himself onto his elbows. It was possible he'd cracked a rib. "And just what purpose does the ever-honorable Cheverley assign my worthless, purity-ruining life?"

"Fatherhood, Ash. You are going to have a child."

THE MYSTERIOUS GUEST seated next to Hester had dark chestnut hair adorned with jewels. Her dress draped across her breasts in the Grecian style the countess had inspired. She was beautiful. Hauntingly beautiful. But the excited fury that lit her eyes left Alicia cold.

"Meet Madame Bianci," Hester replied. "Your lover's former mistress."

"Hester," Alicia breathed, "what have you done?"

Madame Bianci assessed Alicia with a jealous glare. After a short perusal, her shoulders relaxed and a slight smile touched her mouth. She'd judged herself superior.

"I am sorry we must meet under these unfortunate circumstances." Her exaggerated accent was of indeterminate origin. "I understand you are considering an arrangement with the Duke of Ashbey."

"With due respect...Madame Bianci, was it? I am doing no such thing."

"No need to draw daggers, my dear," the Madame continued. "No one in the world understands as well as I." She sighed. "Ash can be thoughtful. Generous, too. His gifts make you think he understands...has a heart."

Ashbey. Ash. He'd said no other lover had called him Ash. Alicia was going to be sick.

"But no." The Madame's lips pinched. "He cultivates with such care only to engender obligation."

"He wants you to feel you owe him," Hester explained.

As if Alicia did not understand. As if she hadn't known from the start. But she hadn't heeded her misgivings, had she? She'd allowed herself to be seduced, not with caresses and pretty gifts, but with the admiration he'd faked.

"Madame, I would never consent to be anyone's mistress. Thank you for your time—"

"The Duke of Ashbey is a villain," the Madam interrupted, calmly removing her glove. She lifted her hand. A jagged scar marred her palm and fingers. "He did this to me the day I told him we were finished."

Alicia stared at the scar, her heart pounding in her throat. *Impossible.* Cold and unkind, yes. But this?

"Do you know the family history?" Madame Bianci asked.

"Of course," Alicia replied.

"His father killed, no matter what the courts decided. Hot blood, too." Madame Bianci's eyes glittered. "No planning. He just..." She snapped her fingers. "A sword through his valet's stomach, right in front of his wife. Smart woman, she ran. No one has heard from her since—not even after her husband died. That tells you how much she thought of her son."

Oh God, Ash.

"I ran, too." Madame Bianci leaned forward. "If you wish to remain unharmed, I suggest you do the same."

"You see, Alicia?" Hester asked. "You simply cannot trust this man."

Alicia turned to Hester. "I cannot believe you would sink this low."

"That child," Hester pointed to Alicia's still-flat belly, "will be shunned without the Stone family's acceptance."

Madame Bianci gasped. "Child?"

"There is no child," Alicia lied.

"I should think not," Madame Bianci said. "Ashbey would never allow bad blood—legitimate or otherwise—into this world. He was always clear on that fact. The line dies with him."

Alicia paled. If true, how far would he go to prevent her from giving birth?

She shook her head.

She knew in her heart this woman's opinion was not one she could trust.

"Again, Madame," she said, "I thank you for your time. I've

never been introduced to the Duke of Ashbey." That much was true. "My Aunt has lost her mind." She slanted a glance to Hester and whispered, "Laudanum."

Hester gasped in indignation.

"I only wished to help." Madame shrugged as she carefully donned her glove. "His wife died in a tragic fire. They say she set the blaze, but perhaps not. If she were with child, a child he did not want..."

Alicia's heart leapt into her throat. "I told you. I have never been introduced to the Duke of Ashbey." That much was true— he'd introduced himself. "Tell her you were mistaken, Aunt Hester. Tell her *now*."

Hester frowned. "I—I—could have misheard."

The Madame shrugged. "Better yet, then." She rose. "I will see myself out."

The Madame sauntered into the hall, retrieved her cloak, and then followed the butler to the back.

"At least," Alicia hissed, "you had sense enough not to bring her through the front door."

Hester's mouth set in a mulish line. "I heard you say Ashbey, I am sure."

"Nothing good comes from listening at keyholes!" She rubbed her head. "Go to bed," Alicia said. "I must think."

"I—I am sorry if I misheard," Hester said. "I had to take drastic action! You wouldn't listen to me."

"You must stop this, Hester. The countess is not going to inherit Astonbury. Neither will we. The estate will go to Simon."

"Simon?"

"Yes, Simon. The captain told me as much. You may cease this nonsense about an heir."

Hester covered her lips.

"Really, Hester, your nephew will hardly force you to the streets."

"Of course not," Hester said. "But what about you? What will Simon do when he learns of your bastard child?"

Alicia swallowed, as the answer suddenly became clear. "He won't. I expect to be long gone."

AFTER AN HOUR of pouring over lists and figures, Alicia constructed a plan. Then, the muffled sound of the night watchman's raised voice brought Alicia to the window. Rain tinged the glass, and her breath mottled her already-limited view.

The watchman approached a dark figure in the square, a shadow of a man that made her shiver. The watchman held up his lamp, and the figure turned.

Ashbey's angled features glowed.

The watchman bowed and backed away. Alicia dropped the curtain.

She placed a protective hand over her belly and sent up a small curse. *Cheverley.* So much for keeping his word. How could she have trusted a man who had given her a false name?

Somewhere amid the thudding of her heart she found her voice, and called for the butler. When he entered, she paused for a moment, stunned at what she was about to do. "There is a man in the square."

The butler's brows rose.

"Retrieve him," she said primly, "please."

His eyebrows went higher. "You wish to bring a vagabond into the house?"

Her back straightened. "That vagabond is the Duke of Ashbey."

"Lady Stone," the butler recovered his usual composure, "why don't you have a seat in the dining room, and I will bring you a nice cup of tea?"

"If you do not go out there and convince the duke to come to the back door, he's going to march right up the front stairs in full view of all the neighbors and—"

The great knocker on the front door clanged. Matching the thud of her heart.

The butler opened the door, asking whom he might announce.

Without a word, the duke limped into the hall, dripping with rain and filling the room with an anger that smoldered like sulfur. A vicious purple bruise left his flesh sagging beneath his right eye.

"If I could take your—" the butler began.

"Leave us," he said.

Ashbey's gaze hadn't left Alicia's face. Even in his state, to see him was a balm she hadn't known she craved.

She tore her eyes away long enough to address the butler. "You may go."

"Lady Stone," the butler cautioned, "if you would permit—"

"Go," the duke boomed.

Alicia concealed her shaking hands. "I will take care of our guest."

The butler bowed in retreat.

"Were you going to tell me?" His voice sent a frightened rush through her blood.

I am no helpless maid to his feudal lord. She strode past him into the parlor. He followed, closing the door.

"Well?"

She swallowed. "I hadn't yet decided."

"You hadn't *decided*?"

Why hadn't she seen it—the dark force that pulsed around him like a curse? Why hadn't she been afraid she'd be consumed?

He would consume her, no matter what choice she made. Even now, she felt her resistance crumbling like a harbor in a hurricane, torn to pieces the way her childhood home had been torn to pieces.

She must stand strong against the storm, even if a feral part of her heart cried out to him just because Ash was near.

She paced the length of the room, trying to find the calm center, but her foundations had been uprooted, her thoughts silenced by the anger that pulsed through the room like a live thing.

He was angry, was he? She was angry, too.

"How dare you come to my door in the middle of the night? The watchman recognized you, no doubt."

"I don't give a damn if the whole street was peering out their windows."

Her eyes narrowed. "Was that your plan? Ruin me and force my hand?"

"Alicia," he said, rough as a gravel path.

"Don't use my name."

"Lady Stone, then, if you prefer." His voice had grown cold. "I believe you owe—"

"Owe? *Owe?* I owe you nothing." She backed away. "All along I *knew* you felt I was your right." A terrible lump refused to move from her throat.

"You *are* my right."

His right? A man who believed so would not hesitate to send away her child.

She shook her head no. "Do you think you have a right to me just because you bought my grief? You are no better than the spectators who bought tickets to see your father's trial."

He jerked back as if he'd been hit. "Not like that, Alicia. Never like that."

"Why did you buy me? What was your plan? To pass a few days indolence, see if you could make the little widow cry?"

His gaze narrowed. His nostrils flared.

She held her brow and shook her head. "I cannot believe I allowed you to bind me. Literally bind me! When I had sworn never to don shackles again! Is that the only way you can feel?"

Blood drained from his face, leaving his cheeks ghostly pale. "Forgive me."

"For which of your sins?"

He drew a ragged breath. "Hubris."

"Hubris?"

His jaw twitched. "I spoke in anger. You owe me nothing. You never owed me anything."

Somehow that was worse.

"The child, Alicia," he said softly. "We must speak of my child."

"Your child?"

He flinched. After a silence he said, "Yes, mine."

As if she would let him near anything innocent and pure. "Actually, not."

"What are you saying?" His voice chilled.

She had wanted to suggest she loved another. She had wanted to hurt him the way he'd hurt her. She could not. "The law assumes the child belongs to Octavius."

"You, who cannot lie, would lie to our child and the world?"

"I would." She lifted her chin. "To protect my child."

"From *me?*"

"Yes, from you!" Her lashes dampened as she struggled to master the wild thing in her chest.

"You know I would not harm a child. *Our* child."

"Do I?"

He shut his eyes, squeezing them closed as if he could make the whole world vanish. An ugly vein pulsed at his temple.

He folded his hands behind his back and bowed. Horribly courtly. Ghastly polite. "I will take my leave."

Oh Lord. This had not been what she wanted. She faltered. *Ashbey. Ash. Give me a reason to trust you.*

He strode back through the door into the hall.

"Ash," she whispered.

"You are perfectly correct, of course. An association with my name would only harm the child."

He squeezed the bridge of his nose, and winced. She lifted her hand.

He stepped away. "I will, of course, provide any funds you require."

"Ash," she whispered again.

"Goodbye, Lady Stone. Good night." He paused at the door. "I never meant—" His voice cracked. He dropped his head. "For three days, you made a broken man feel whole."

CHAPTER 14

*A*sh stared at his study ceiling and fingered the collar of his Banyan. A trace of Alicia's scent provoked longing sharp as pain.

Not only did she not want him, she'd gone so far as to return his banyan.

Would that he could go back to the days when his chest was barren, containing nothing but infertile, salted dirt. Now he was overwhelmed with sentiments. The kind of sentiments that did not grow in neat, cultivated rows, but stuck out in every direction, like the blasted thorny weeds on the drive to Wisterley.

Death would come eventually. Not soon enough for Ash.

He'd tried to protect her from his gloom. He'd tried and failed. Now she was convinced she must protect their child from him.

His one consolation?

She finally understood how dangerous he was. Not much a consolation, truth be told. More like a dagger to his chest. Unfortunately, that kind of dagger couldn't make him bleed.

The door opened. He rolled onto his side.

"Made a muck of it, has he?" Hurtheven asked.

"A muck of what?" Chev questioned back.

"The woman."

"How did you know there was a woman?" Chev snorted. "I thought Kent was discreet."

"Kent is," Hurtheven replied. "He didn't tell me a thing. But you just confirmed my suspicion." A back was slapped. "Cease your grimace. Every problem always comes down to a woman."

Chev snorted. "Hyperbole isn't helpful, Hurtheven."

"There is not a woman," Ash said aloud. Not anymore.

"I beg to differ," Chev said. "I've only just seen Lady Stone."

"Lady Stone, huh?" Hurtheven exclaimed. "You *are* a devil, Ash."

Ash scowled. He needn't be told. He knew.

"Well," Chev said, "if he really is a devil, the antichrist is expected in approximately eight months."

Hurtheven whistled. "Bad go, my friend."

"I tried to make amends," Ash replied. "She does not want anything to do with me. She's *afraid* of me. Maybe her fears are well-founded. She and the child will be better off where I cannot taint them by association."

Hurtheven hummed thoughtfully. "You almost have to admire Ash's commitment to self-flagellation."

"Dates back all the way to Eton," Cheverley agreed. "Possibly even before."

"Thunder-faced and forlorn, that is our Ash. ...Although, are we being fair? He never elicited our pity."

"True," Cheverley replied. "He actually believes it noble to remain alone."

"Have you been tainted?" Hurtheven asked.

"No. You?" Chev countered.

"Not that I can say." Hurtheven tapped his chin. "Perhaps we should ask Lady Stone?"

"Stay away from Lady Stone," Ash replied.

"I believe that is what we told you at the start," Hurtheven replied. "If you cannot listen, you should learn."

Ash groaned. "Is there no one else you can bother, Hurtheven?"

"Did you hear his tone?" Hurtheven asked. "He's elevated his usual menace."

"You did give him the name Hades."

"Well, yes," Hurtheven preened. "I am a brilliant judge of character, there's no disputing that."

"*Go away.*" Ash kept his eyes firmly closed. One did not engage Hurtheven. Not when he was in this humor.

Hurtheven *tsked*. "He hasn't been this bad since the fire."

"In his defense," Chev supplied, "losing one's wife, father and home is apt to make one melancholy."

"He was melancholy before. But this... This is simple indulgence."

Do not engage.

"Arrogance," Hurtheven continued, "of the highest form."

"You would know arrogance." Ash opened one eye. "It is hardly conceit to protect others."

"Is that what you are doing?" Chev asked.

Yes, it was. Wasn't it?

"Say, Chev, on a scale of woebegone indolence to despondent wallow, where does our hero fall?"

"The needle leans heavily toward wallow."

"You two have no idea—" Ash started. Chev's raised brow made him pause.

Hurtheven hit Ash's shoulder with his knee. "Get up, fool. I am here to mount a rescue. I haven't all day, you know. Not even for you."

"No rescue is required."

Hurtheven clapped his hands and then rubbed them together. "I'd appreciate if one of you would pour me a drink so we can get started."

Ash sat up. "Why is it that you always barge into my rooms and demand a drink?"

Hurtheven grinned. "Because you buy fine tipple of course. Much better than I can afford."

Ash lifted a brow. "You are rich beyond measure."

Hurtheven shrugged. "Much more than I am willing to pay, then."

"I'll serve," Ash said. "But only because I find myself craving something strong."

With difficulty, Ash went over to the cabinet and then distributed healthy pours. He sat down with a sigh and drank in a healthy measure.

"You confronted her, I take it?" Chev asked.

Ash gazed into the soft, brown liquid and nodded. "She told me she'd do anything to keep her child safe."

"Sounds reasonable," Hurtheven said.

Ash glanced up. "From *me*."

"Well, then!" Chev shook his head. "You must have made quite an impression."

"The bruises you gave me did not improve my appearance," Ash replied.

"Doubtless." Chev leaned forward. "What *were* you thinking?"

Ash's head whipped up. "I bloody well wasn't *thinking*. I went over there just after you left."

"You were bleeding, for God's sake!"

Ash grimaced. "You'd know something about that, wouldn't you?"

"Yes, well," Chev replied. "You deserved a beating, didn't you?"

Ash looked away. "Our arrangement was for three nights." His breath caught. "I never meant to cause her harm."

"Well"—Hurtheven raised his brows—"what happened on the final morning?"

"Kent saw her off."

Chev and Hurtheven exchanged a speaking glance.

He knew he'd been a fool. He should have fought with all his might. But even if they'd managed to wrest a time of happiness, the end would have been the same.

What hurt most was that she believed he would harm their child. That he was as mad as his father.

"I am not mad," he said.

"Oh?" Chev replied. "You pursued a woman you'd never laid eyes on before. Then you abandoned her without so much as a farewell. And after you found out she was with child, you accosted her in her own home." He leaned in. "It all sounds perfectly rational to me."

"It wasn't...rational, I know." Ash frowned. "But neither was it the work of madness. When I saw her—" An image of Alicia rose in his mind—so beautiful, so untouchable, so fine.

What the devil was happening to his eyes? He shook his head and wetness seeped between his lashes.

"Damnation." He pinched the bridge of his nose.

"Good God," Chev said. "You love her."

"He loves her." Hurtheven hit the arm of his chair. "And yet, he let her go."

"I am protecting her! Chev told me she had scandal enough." He propped his elbows on his knees and dropped his head. "She said I wasn't any better than the slime that bought tickets to my father's trial."

"She said *that*?" Chev asked.

Ash winced. "I may have implied she owed me."

Chev clucked his tongue. "You deserved worse, then."

"Don't I know," Ash sighed.

"Come, now," Hurtheven scoffed. "Something real is at stake, here. *A child.* You had a mad father. Her husband was a cheat. So? These things aren't rare. What is rare is you, weeping into your scotch—finally in love."

Ash looked up. Hurtheven's face twisted with bitterness.

"I loathe you both for finding love." Hurtheven's gaze moved to Chev. "I'll loath you both even more if you let it go to waste."

"What if," Ash's voice cracked, "she ends up dead, like Rachel?"

Hurtheven's gaze softened. "Stop right there. Enough is enough, Ash. You are a league past wallow, now. Are you to drown in despair? Where's the spirit you had when you claimed your father's name? Lady Stone has seen your darkness. Reveal your light."

"I have no light."

"Who—as soon as he was old enough—protected the servants, ensuring anyone who wished to leave found a position in a household where they would be safe?"

Ash frowned. "You?"

Hurtheven shrugged. "At *your* request."

"Who," Chev asked, "made frequent trips to visit my wife, making sure she had everything she needed? Yes—I know about that."

"She is a good woman," Ash replied. "You would have done the same for me, if I'd had a wife in a similar position."

"I *will* do the same for you," Chev replied. "I will plead your case."

"My case?" Ash asked.

"You plan to marry her, of course," Hurtheven said.

He hadn't.

He hadn't, not because he did not want to marry Alicia, but because he had not dared to believe she'd agree. And that was before he'd poured salt in her wounds.

"What if I break her?" Ash whispered.

"She survived the admiral," Hurtheven answered.

"I broke even Bianci—" Ash started.

"Bianci? Miss White?" Hurtheven shook his head. "Bianci clawed her way from a job as a costume girl to be the prima donna of the stage on pure ambition. You may have stung her pride, but you did not break her. She left you for someone with more shine. And why shouldn't she have left? You didn't care if she stayed or not."

Ash frowned. Was that true? He'd been put out when she'd left. Mostly because she'd been vicious. But he hadn't been heart-broken. And, she had left him for someone better, hadn't she? A Prince, no less.

"Bianci and her Prince are still...?" he asked.

Hurtheven nodded. "Besotted."

Maybe he did not ruin *everything* he touched.

"Do you think Lady Stone would agree to be my wife?" Ash asked.

"*I* wouldn't marry anyone who left their home a wreck." Hurtheven patted Ash's knee. "It is time, I think, for you to put Wisterley to rights."

"Wisterley..." Ash's voice trailed as he remembered Alicia's words.

The lonely turrets became sad. I wished with all my being that someone would come along and see the beauty there. That someone would rescue the ruin, love the house for all it could be and make it whole once again. Make it a home.

"...Wisterley is a wreck. No one besides the Kents would dare set foot within the walls."

"The servants I hired would return, if you asked." Hurtheven stretched his legs. "And they are a crippling expense. Absolutely crippling."

Ash snorted. "You aren't needling me because of the expense."

"Not *just* because of the expense," Hurtheven said. "I am selfish to my core. I want you to join society."

"Weren't you just accusing *me* of being selfish?" Ash asked.

Hurtheven shrugged. "Selfishness is part of my nature. It is not part of yours."

Ash swallowed. "What if I restore Wisterley, and she still does not want me?"

"That," Cheverley replied, "is a risk you must take."

"*You* have work you must do. You have a special license to procure and," Hurtheven lifted his brows, "a great deal of construction to plan."

The wraith-like specter of hope crystalized. Wisterley, a home. Alicia by his side. His breath slowed.

"It seems so impossible," he said.

"Faith," Hurtheven replied.

Faith. Yes, faith. And what did faith do? It made the impossible possible. It brought what had been in darkness into the light.

"By the way," Chev said, "the sooner we implement a plan, the better. After you have won your lady, I'm planning to take *your* advice."

"And go home to Penelope?" Ash asked.

Chev nodded. "If she wants me as I am."

"She'll want you," Hurtheven replied. "Trust me."

What had been lost between them slipped back into place—a brotherly bond sealed.

CHAPTER 15

*A*licia awaited for the countess in Astonbury's morning room.

The room had been dull, if she properly recalled. Since then, it had come into alignment with its name. Admittedly, the countess had fine taste. The walls were a deep, cheerful yellow, and coordinating striped satin covered the stuffed chairs. The countess was one of the most oft-painted women, yet the tables and walls were adorned with images not of her, but of Octavius.

All except one.

Alicia set down the bundle of letters and approached that painting—the same one she'd seen the day of the funeral. A rueful smile touched her lips. She wasn't surprised the countess had commissioned the original. The countess had carefully cultivated Octavius's fame from the time the two had met. She'd also made dreary Astonbury both a home for Octavius while he lived, and now a shrine.

The countess had, in fact, made Octavius a much better wife.

Where Alicia had seen a selfish, sullen man, the countess had seen only a hero.

Oh, the countess and Octavius had rows.

From the accusations and apologies that appeared in the letters, far more rows than she and Octavius had ever had. But, in her heart, the countess had believed Octavius was the most interesting, powerful, loving man she'd ever known. And, Octavius had clearly felt the same of the countess.

Octavius had never looked at her the way he looked at the countess. Not even when he'd been ardent and romantic and wooing with charm.

But the duke had looked at her that way. The duke had gazed at her with awe, as if she were a woman of infinite worth. Such a look seduced. Such a look branded.

...you made a broken man feel whole.

An aching sense of loss rattled, like wind through dried leaves. She missed the duke. They'd only spent three nights together, and yet, as his child grew within her body, she missed him more every day.

If things hadn't gone wrong, if, instead of letting her go, he'd asked her to stay, would she be able to make a home for them both as the countess had made a home for Octavius?

Of course.

Although with fewer portraits. And less yellow.

She turned as the countess rushed into the room, everything about her a flutter. She had always been a little breathtaking, the countess. Even now, though years and grief had taken their toll, the portrait-come-to-life effect left Alicia speechless.

The countess saw Alicia and froze, suspending them both in a hazy uncertainty that could have ended either with consolation or bitter recrimination. Then, the countess curtseyed, with her head bowed. The countess, who clearly out-ranked Alicia.

She approached Alicia with her arms outstretched. Truly, she was impossible to dislike.

"I am *so* honored by your presence," the countess gushed.

Alicia believed her sincere. "Thank you for seeing me."

She held Alicia's hands. Her touch was warm, her famed eyes, full of concern. "How *awful* this has been. Have you been sleeping? I haven't. Not a wink." Her gaze drifted to the largest of the paintings. "I miss him so." She broke into a sob. A rush of tears followed. Then, they were gone as quickly as they'd come. "Oh dear, I *am* sorry. How selfish of me. You, of course, miss him, too."

Painfully, not.

Alicia had grieved for him long before he died. But she would never have wished his death. "I am sorry for the Nation's loss." Oddly enough, she was sorry for the countess's loss, too.

The countess's tears renewed. "So tragic. *So* unfair." Her eyes widened. "Unfair to us both, of course."

"Yes." On those points, Alicia could agree.

The countess inhaled, dropped one of Alicia's hands, and led her to the couch. "The Admiralty has been wretched to me, as I am certain they have been to you. All but for that one, nice man."

"Captain Smith?" Alicia ventured, smoothing her skirts to sit.

"Oh yes! But of course, you know him, too. He's to come here today." The countess clapped. "Oh! *Oh!* I've had a marvelous idea. You should stay, and we will see him together."

Wouldn't Cheverley be surprised? "Thank you, but no. I cannot stay. There is a coach that returns to the city in a little more than an hour."

The countess looked horrified. "You mustn't leave so soon! And not when we have so much to celebrate. I was wretched. Just wretched. I didn't know what to do. And now, everything is going to be beautifully settled."

Alicia frowned. "Settled?"

"Yes, of course! Why it happened nearly a week ago. Don't you know?"

Astonbury was to go to Simon. Clearly, that was *not* the news animating the countess.

"A *trust* has been set up for Octavia." The countess squeezed Alicia's hand and made a happy noise. "Can you believe?"

A trust? Alicia carefully chose her words. "The Admiralty came around, then."

"The Admiralty." The Countess looked as if she'd tasted raw meat. "They wanted nothing to do with my poor Octavia, even though caring for her was her father's express wish."

The countess seemed to realize what she said, and withdrew her hands. She had never admitted to Alicia that Octavia belonged to Octavius. Then again, seeing them both, who would have doubted?

"Countess..." Strange that she should wish to reassure this creature who had stolen her husband. "...I could never begrudge a child their"—the last word caught—"father."

Her eyes stung. *Ash.*

"Oh! *Oh.* You are too kind." The countess pressed her hand-kerchief against her lips with a sob. "You've always been too kind."

Not always. "What was it you were saying about a trust?"

The countess brightened. "Oh yes, of course. Captain Smith set up the trust." She frowned. "Not really Captain Smith, though. His friend. An Earl. Or was it a duke?" The countess pursed her lips as she tried to recall. "The terms are what count, anyway. Simon is to have custody. Terrible thing, but that was never in doubt. I cannot. Can you imagine? A child's own mother."

A terrible fear passed through Alicia's heart. "That is true of all women, I believe."

"That is exactly what the solicitor said. But the trust will help Simon provide for Octavia, so she will not be a burden. And Simon has promised that I am to have her daily care."

"Who is trustee?"

"There are to be two. The Captain's friend the duke—yes, he was most certainly a duke—and Simon." The countess sighed. "They have both agreed to allow Octavia and I to go on as we have." Her eyes filled again. "I do not know what I would do without my sweet child."

"I am happy for you," Alicia said slowly. *It couldn't be.*

"Thank you." The countess caught up her hands. "*Thank* you."

"Octavia is fortunate to have such a generous benefactor."

"Oh yes. As fortunate as she can be, under the circumstances. Captain Smith brought him to meet me. I was frightened at first. I'd heard he was mad..."

Alicia stopped breathing. Perhaps it couldn't be, but it was.

"Oh, do not worry. The duke wasn't mad at all. I should know better than to heed nasty rumors."

"Did he..." Alicia swallowed. "Did he say why he'd done something so generous?"

The countess nodded. "He said it would be cruel to part a mother and child."

Ashbey. Her own tears spilled forth.

"Oh, dear." The countess fluttered her hands.

"I'm fine." She wasn't. "I—I really must be going." She stood and retrieved the packet. "I came to return something that belongs to you."

"My letters," the countess breathed, as if Alicia had been holding gold. "Bless you! Oh, bless you."

The countess became so consumed by the letters, she permitted Alicia to leave without much protest. Alicia slipped away.

Outside, the sun was bright and warm in the Spring sky, and the sight somehow comforted. She had almost reached the end of the drive when a carriage turned into the gates. Glossy and dark —the Admiralty attempting to be discreet.

The coachman lifted the window that looked down into the box. "Right," he yelled. The carriage slowed. The door swung open and two men peered out.

She'd expected Cheverley. She had not expected Simon.

"Hello, Alicia." Simon looked guilty.

My, he'd changed. He was looking more and more like Octavius. "It's wonderful to see you, dear." Three years past,

Simon would have jumped into her arms. This tidy young man was much more reserved. "And such a surprise."

"Yes." Simon winced. "I imagine you are surprised to find me here...and aggrieved."

"You are mistaken. If you have come to visit your niece, I heartily approve." Alicia's gaze slid to Cheverley. "The countess told me about the trust. Be good to Octavia, Simon. Your brother loved her."

Simon exhaled. "You're a good sort."

"Yes, well." Alicia looked away. "Aunt Hester will be your challenge."

Simon shifted his feet. "I haven't yet been to call."

Alicia raised a brow. "She would love to see you."

Simon nodded.

"Go on," Alicia urged. "Go visit your family."

"If you wait," Cheverley spoke for the first time, "you would be welcome to join us on the return."

Alicia shook her head no.

"Lord Stone, you do as she bids." Cheverley opened the door and hopped down from the carriage. "I will accompany Lady Stone to the posting inn."

Simon agreed. Alicia covered her face as the carriage wheels kicked up dirt. When the dust had settled, she turned to Cheverley.

"Did Ashbey do this for me?"

"For you? No." Cheverley squinted at something over her shoulder. "Because of you? Almost certainly." He looked back. "Simon is young yet. Easily influenced. I was concerned about placing Octavia in Simon's care."

"Why didn't you set up the trust?"

"Captain Smith does not exist." Cheverley cocked his head. "Ashbey never intended you to know about the trust. Some rubbish about not wanting you to think he was trying to buy your good will."

She looked away. "The countess is not the soul of discretion."

"Well," Cheverley chuckled, "no one expected you to visit your husband's mistress."

Alicia shrugged. "I had letters belonging to her."

"You've a good heart."

Alicia's lips twisted. "So I keep hearing."

"The question is—is your heart big enough to allow Ashbey a second chance?"

She frowned. "Why are you defending him?"

"He's loyal, for one. I've been gone for six long years. He's taken care of my wife, helped with my son. He need not have done either."

Alicia's eyes stung.

"He believes himself cursed. He believes he will destroy anyone who is close to him. Nonsense, of course."

"Are you saying he was protecting me?"

Cheverley nodded.

She touched her brow where Ash's lips had rested at the end of their final night. *…you made a broken man feel whole.*

"What if he takes my child?"

"Would a man who set up a trust so a bastard could remain with her mother part his own child from hers?"

"I don't know." Alicia frowned "You didn't see his eyes."

Cheverley's gaze softened. "You are going to have to decide. But remember, you are not without a friend in me."

Alicia's heart warmed. "Thank you, Lord Cheverley."

CHAPTER 16

$\mathcal{N}$ow that Simon had returned, Alicia relinquished her place. Once she'd made the decision, all that had seemed impossible became easy, and in less than a fortnight, her transition was complete.

With Lord Cheverley's help, she'd arranged to rent rooms—the same rooms on the third floor of the bakery near Brighton, where she had spent time with Octavius. Now that she was settled, Cheverley was to set up a meeting with the duke.

When she confronted him, it would not be in weakness and supplication.

But when she arrived at her new lodgings yesterday eve, a package awaited. The Banyan. She clutched the note in her hands.

This is a prized possession, given to me by Chev. But, it is yours, now. Keep it. Perhaps you can show it to your child—a memento of his father. I'd rather, however, you return to me.

She placed her hand over her softly swelling belly and fixed her eyes on the ruined castle she'd once loved. Workmen swarmed about the place. looking, from this distance, like an army of tiny ants.

Someone was finally setting it to rights.

"I don't know why you wished to come back," the baker's wife huffed. "This place hasn't ever been a haven for the content." Mrs. Wilton joined her at the window. "Though now that there is work being done on the castle, we all hope..." She sighed. "The young one was a good boy, you know. Quiet-like. Good to us too, until she came. We saw him less and less, and then, the fire." She shook her head. "The old duke got what he deserved, some say. He did it, you know, acquitted or not."

Prickles went up Alicia's back. "You—you never spoke of the family."

Mrs. Wilton looked sheepish. "Superstition. No one would speak of the family, less they too be cursed."

Alicia swallowed hard. "What is the name of the castle?"

"Why Wisterley castle, of course. The seat of the dukes of Ashbey."

She masked her surprise with a light cough.

Could it be? Had she slept in the same castle that had captured her imagination?

Alicia Studied the castle and the wide, bare drive leading up to it. "But I don't see the blackthorn that grows along the drive."

The baker's wife looked confused. Then, her brow cleared. "What you see is the new drive. Another drive approaches from the south and ends at the oldest part of the keep—that's where the blackthorn grows."

Her heartbeat began to gallop. "Where can I hire a carriage?"

"At the inn." Mrs. Wilton frowned. "But it is doubtful one could be had on a Sunday morn."

Alicia couldn't breathe. "I—I need to walk."

"Are you sure?" the baker's wife asked. "You look a bit peaked, and—"

But Alicia was already tripping down the stairs. She trudged along the primary street, heedless of the light rain misting the air. She had been to hell and back. A little rain was no cause for hesitation.

Actually, she preferred the rain.

Who needed things to be lovely all the time? Without the rain, the flowers wouldn't grow. And without the dark of night, sleep could not renew. And without one devil duke, her heart would still be broken, and her belly barren.

Without allowing herself to decide whether her actions were right or wrong, reasoned or mad, she headed toward the castle.

Halfway up the drive, she paused, turning to face the sea. Churning water reflected a greyish hue that bled into low-hanging clouds. She rested there, and just as she had so many times before, she cast her worries into the arms of the deep.

She sent out into the sea wishes for Octavius's eternal peace. Wishes for relief of the countess's suffering. Wishes that the Stone family would find the strength and courage to face their future, whatever that may bring. And, finally, she made a solemn wish and promise to herself—if she were lucky enough to survive childbirth, she would love her child as much as she loved her child's father.

With the roar of the waves in her ears, she experienced perfect peace.

Not peace as she had imagined it—placid and angelic—but a deeper peace. Peace that existed in the heart of turmoil. Peace that was the knowledge that life springs only from messy chaos.

Darkness always precedes light.

She returned to her climb, marveling at the unpredictable nature of chance.

Fate had drawn her back to the very castle that had occupied her thoughts and she never once guessed. She'd even told Ashbey about the castle—why hadn't he revealed the truth?

Her feet made crunching noises against the gravel as the incline steepened. Then she turned the corner. From this expanse, she could see the whole castle—the tower in the back where she'd stayed, and the front, which had once been magnificent. Even the shell was ornate enough to steal her breath.

What a terrible loss.

Coming back must have been painful for Ashbey, and yet, from the start, he'd wanted *her* here. *I want you in my bed.* She placed her hand over her belly and blinked away the tears.

This had once been a place of beauty. There was beauty even now in the ruin. And maybe...

She wanted to trust the light. Wanted to trust with all her heart.

She remained in place as the clouds parted, and the sun shined down into the roofless rooms.

RESTLESSLY, Ashbey headed for the stables. When he'd promised to trust Cheverley, he hadn't considered just how wrong inaction would feel. He should be down at the Baker's house, on his knees, begging his wife to return.

Well, on a fine point, she was not yet his wife, but she would be.

He hoped.

The signed license sat snug in his pocket. The bishop had not been happy. But any of his misgivings not dispelled by Ash's professed devotion had been assuaged by Ash's generous donation.

Still, he could not marry a woman if she did not agree.

He'd done nothing to convince her to remain by his side—nothing to prove he could become a worthy husband. A worthy father.

He turned on his heel and shielded his eyes. A mist fell, but even so, the morning sun brightened all. And, in the middle of the tableau, was a lone female figure on the path. *Alicia?*

It couldn't be Alicia.

But it was.

"Alicia!" he called as he ran, her name broken by his labored breathing. "Alicia!"

"Ash?" She looked confused. Maybe frightened.

He forced himself to stop.

"Please," he held an arm against the cramp in his side, and continued to run. "Please don't go."

"Go?"

He grasped her by the shoulders. She *was* real! "You have no idea how much I've missed..." He choked on the final word.

ALICIA WAS CAUGHT up against Ash's body.

"Alicia," he repeated between wracking breaths, "Alicia. You are here. You are really here."

"Shh," she crooned. "Yes. I am here now." She didn't dare touch his face, so she fisted her hands in the fabric of his waistcoat, holding him close. "I am fine. Just tired." So, so tired.

He touched his forehead to hers. "And you must never leave."

"I would have stayed the last time," her voice quivered, "if you had asked."

"I tried. I swear I tried."

"What do you mean?"

"The coach was a league ahead. It kept appearing then disappearing in the fog." His Adam's apple moved as he swallowed. "I thought he'd stay on the less traveled road, so I went in that direction. By the time I realized my mistake, you were hours ahead. I convinced myself I'd been wrong to go after you."

Fog collected inside her mind, but she *felt* that day. The feeling he was near—the sense of madness. "You followed the coach?"

"Yes," he said. He kissed her cheeks, her nose and her forehead. "But I lost you."

He had come. He hadn't abandoned her. Could it possibly be true?

"My lady," he breathed.

"My lady," she whispered. "I never became accustomed to being addressed as such."

He smoothed her hair away from her face. "How about Your Grace?"

She blinked. "Pardon?"

"I—I may never be fully whole, but I entrust my broken self to you with a promise of love and loyalty for all my days. Forgive me, Alicia. I love you. I love you, and I want you to be my wife."

"Oh Ash."

He bit his lip. "I don't know what that sound in your voice means."

She turned her head and placed her ear on his heart. "Ask me what I hear."

"What do you hear?"

"Love." She drew back and cupped his neck. She smiled a weepy smile. "If you'll have me—us, I mean—then yes. I love you, Ashbey—body, heart, and soul."

She yelped as Ash lifted her into his arms.

"What are you doing?"

"I am taking you to church, so you can repeat that promise before God—and the vicar."

She started to laugh. "You are mad."

"No—finally not."

"You can't carry me the whole way down to the village," she said, though he was doing just that. "You are carrying two."

It was his turn to shush. He told her to rest. She gave up arguing and tucked her head beneath his chin, snuggling close. It was the best feeling she'd ever had.

～

THE CHURCHYARD WAS full of carriages. Ash didn't care. He kicked open the door. A child let the bell rope fall. The congregation, who had been preparing to leave, collectively gasped.

"If you would, vicar. I have a special license from the Archbishop of Canterbury."

Shouting sounded from the yard. Then, Cheverley rushed inside the church. "Lud, Ash, you are hard to follow." He winced. "Sorry, vicar. Name in vain, and all that." He looked over his shoulder. "Hurtheven! You had better hurry."

Hurtheven joined them.

"Alicia, soon-to-be Duchess of Ashbey, may I present, His Grace, the Duke of Hurtheven?"

"Pleased, Your Grace," Alicia said.

"Honored, my dear," Hurtheven replied.

"Lord Cheverley, what are you doing here?" Alicia asked.

"We've been here since you came," Cheverley replied.

"Although why we are here," Hurtheven added, "depends very much on how you answered Ash. If yes, then, we are here to celebrate. If no, then we are here to console." His eyes moved between them. "Looks like a yes. Put down your wife-to-be, Ash."

Ash set Alicia on her feet, keeping one arm firmly about her waist.

"Enough pleasantries." Hurtheven tugged his waistcoat. "We've a wedding to attend."

After some confusion, vows were exchanged and the register was signed.

Voices rose to a clamor as Ash broke with convention and kissed his duchess.

For the first time in his life, Ash didn't mind the gossip. From this day on, when people talked of the Duke of Ashbey, instead of whispers of madness and murder, there would be merry tales of a duke and duchess in love.

EPILOGUE

*H*er Grace, the Duchess of Ashbey, watched from the window as her husband directed their son, Phillip, Lord Delmare, into the Duke of Hurtheven's open landeau. Just this morning, Ash and Alicia had reached accord, as a result, at the grand age of three, Delmare received permission to climb the carriage step without holding onto his father's hand.

This very serious honor informed the wee one's stature—he held his chin level to the ground, and his little spine, perfectly straight. Alicia suppressed a giggle.

At Ash's side, a nurse carefully placed Alicia's daughter, Lady Felicia—a name chosen because Ash had used it the first time they'd met—into the cradle Hurtheven had made of his arms.

Hurtheven leaned over the babe, attempting to make the eleven-month-old smile with exaggerated expressions. Felicia grabbed Hurtheven's chin. As he kissed her tiny fingers, her musical baby-laugh wafted through the window, open to the crisp September air.

Hurtheven was not as immune to the children's charms as he sometimes liked to profess.

"We'll return after the fashionable hour," Hurtheven spoke to Ash.

"Take care of them," Ash replied.

"I always do," Hurtheven answered.

"Go! Go!" Phillip said with a scowl.

Ash leaned into the carriage and whispered something into Phillip's ear. Phillip frowned, then nodded, inching his way back into the seat. He folded his hands—a deceptively angelic posture. Hurtheven was in for an adventure today.

Alicia turned away from the window. Her children were safe with Hurtheven, though she suspected his motive for taking them had little to do with an overwhelming desire to visit the Serpentine's ducks. She held the collar of Ashbey's banyan closed as she wandered to the bed and reclined on the mattress.

Judging by the racket coming from the stairwell, Ash was ascending the stairs two steps at a time. Naturally, he was out of breath when he opened the door. A roguishly delicious lock of hair spilled over his forehead. He closed and locked the door.

Alicia leaned toward her husband, a languid and spontaneous response to his presence. "You know why Hurtheven takes them, don't you?"

Ash worked his fingers into his cravat, loosening the knot. "Because we have the two most charming children in all of London?"

"True." Alicia's heart glowed. There had never been a prouder Papa. "But, no."

Ash pulled the cravat out from his collar, and then shrugged out of his coat. "...To provide us a few hours of peace, then."

Lud, those forearms. Those *hands*. She sighed. "No."

Ash leaned on the wall next to the bed. "I give up. Why does Hurtheven bother himself with our children?"

"Because young ladies stop and coo at Felicia," Alicia lifted a brow, "and lean down to exclaim over wee Delmare."

Ash grinned. "Seen though his farce, have you? Clever

duchess." He lifted himself from the wall with the smooth ease of a man aware of his allure. "You inspired his artful use of the children, you know."

"Me?"

Ash hooked his thumbs into the waist of his trousers. "He discovered our children's propensity to encourage feminine conversation during your highly-praised house party at Wisterley."

"Our house party *was* a marvelous success, wasn't it?"

"All due to you. I am very proud. Proud and appreciative." He caressed her face. "But far be it from me to allow Hurtheven's selfishness to go to waste."

Alicia curved her lips in seductive invitation. "A few hours of peace—is that what you have in mind, Ash?"

His eyes gleamed with wicked intent. "I'm more plunder than peace, truth be told."

"Well, then." Alicia threw her legs over the side of the bed. "How do you plan to despoil?"

"I was just thinking," Ash cocked his head, "how very long it's been since you've worn *the dress*."

"The dress..." Alicia bit her lip and creased her brow. "The dress with the tiny pearl buttons that take an age to unfasten?"

Ash shuddered. "Not that one." He parted her knees with his leg.

"Oh!" She glanced up through her lashes, all innocence. "You must mean the dress with the red lace."

"Mmm." His face relaxed with indulgent recollections. "I like that dress, but I love..."

She dropped his banyan from her shoulders. Cool air titillated her breasts, fully exposed above the transparent, diaphanous layers falling from the gathered waist. "This dress?"

Ash's cheeks darkened, his eyes dilated.

His wife worked the buttons of his falls. "I love it when you look at me that way."

Ash hardened beneath her fingers before he caught her wrists in his hands.

"I know a few other things you love."

"You do, do you?"

Ash sunk to his knees. "Absolutely." Placing his lips against her breasts, he proceeded to prove his point.

Alicia laughed, throaty and low. "What did I ever do to deserve you?"

"My darling duchess," he said, "the debt is entirely mine."

THE END

EXCERPT FROM HIS DUCHESS AT EVENTIDE

Lovers reunited, a dukedom reclaimed—the Regency meets the Odyssey

Devastated physically and emotionally by seven years of war, a shipwreck, and six years in the captivity of a brutal pirate, Lord Cheverley, son of the Duke of Ithwick, returns to England to find that the courts have declared him dead, and his wife is entertaining suitors. Should he demand his rightful place, disrupting his family's lives, or should he return to sea, seeking vengeance against the pirate? He sets out to find the answer in disguise.

Penelope once believed in love, but then the man who swept her off her feet deserted her, leaving her and her unborn child utterly alone. Now a widow, she will do anything to protect her son, including enlisting the aid of a mysterious sea captain to uncover the true intentions of her devious suitors. When the captain awakens something in Penelope she thought long dead, she begins to suspect he is no stranger. But, as they peel back the layers of a deadly plot, can this broken family heal their wounds in time to save what really matters?

Book Two of the Mythic Duke Trilogy: His Duchess at Eventide

His Duchess at Eventide is a full length novel of approximately 70 thousand words

Chapter One

November 1805

Wind whipped Captain Lord Cheverley's improvised sail against his raft's mast. Salted sea-spray stung his lips and gusts roared in his ears. Using his shoulder, he wiped rain from his eyes and then re-wedged the paddle between his left arm and leg. Thighs straining, he gripped the groaning rudder.

He hadn't survived the unspeakable—seven years of war, a shipwreck, the loss of his right arm below the elbow, and six excruciating years of captivity—only to fail now.

Had he?

Wine-dark depths did not defer to long-serving officers of the Royal Navy. Frothy white waves were indifferent to sons of dukes. And life-hungry storms didn't give a damn if they stripped wives of their husbands, or sons of their fathers.

Penelope. Thaddeus. Vast emptiness yawned. Instinctively, he beseeched the heavens. Please. I must survive.

No god answered, only darkness without direction, no land, no guiding stars. The blank, shifting water beneath promised death—the same, slow demise that had claimed the lives of Chev's fellow seamen stationed with him on the HMS Defiance.

That gale, too, had materialized as if summoned by Poseidon's trident, without warning and yet powerful enough to devour his sixty-four-gun ship. Rocks like rusted knives protruded from a deadly shoal. Waves thundered without reprieve, breaking the Defiance into pieces unfit for kindling. And his ship's end had been only the beginning of his nightmare.

Tu n'es rien. You are nothing. Je possède chaque partie de tu, maintenant. I own every part of you, now.

His raft listed. He spit over the side.

How much adversity could a man face before he surrendered to annihilation's mercy? How god-damned much?

The wind bellowed. Siren whispers sounded, sensing weakness—supplicate, surrender, submit.

What did he have to offer the world he'd left behind? He'd thought he'd return a hero. Instead, he was broken in body and soul. If he yielded to the storm, would it not be kinder to his family and a just restitution for his sins?

Memories feathered through his thoughts. His face buried in the softness of Penelope's hair. Her fingers, drifting in soothing circles against the small of his back.

He inhaled deep, straining against invisible bonds and roaring back into the wind. He cursed fate. He cursed God. He cursed the pirate witch who'd kept him captive. Then, he cursed himself.

His anger crystalized in breath, clouding the chilled air. He'd escaped captivity, darkness, restraints. Zephyr's winds and Poseidon's waves demanded the final say, but he would not give up without a fight.

Not tonight.

The bundle strapped across his back held what little remained of hung beef and brandy. His cask of fresh water ran low, but he had enough to last another day.

He smothered his weakness, gritted his teeth, and held fast to the rudder.

He'd survive.

He'd survive on the pure need for vengeance.

For years, while Penelope labored to transform her husband's estate, Pensteague House, into a haven, she'd done her best to ignore the specter of neighboring Ithwick Manor, her husband's birthplace. At her worst, she'd wished the house and grounds would simply wither away. Then, however, the duke had been hale, his heir, Piers, alive, and she and her son superfluous to the duchy.

Now, everything had changed, and light filtering through the ducal library's windows chastised her for those fancies—the carpets were worn, the centuries-old relics, dust-laden, and a must-heavy scent burned inside the bridge of her nose. Hour by listless hour, time had been devouring what was left of her husband's boyhood world. And Ithwick's slow demise provided none of her hoped-for triumph.

Still, having done her duty, called on the duke, and reported on Thaddeus's education and care—not that His Grace had appeared to understand a word—she itched to leave this place full of ghosts and greed, mother to the heir or not.

Mrs. Renton—the duke's devoted housekeeper, and one of the few Ithwick residents Penelope trusted—wrung her liver-spotted hands.

"You must stay here at Ithwick," Mrs. Renton said, her pale eyes wide. "The duchy is without a duchess. The duke has lost his sense. Thaddeus remains too young to assume an heir's duties, and I am certain those...those..." Mrs. Renton gestured to the window, "...men mean to destroy everything that's left!"

Moving to the window, Penelope's gaze found the duke's closest male relatives apart from her son. The elder was Mr. Anthony, who, as a descendant of the last duke's brother, was next in line to inherit after Penelope's son. The younger was a more recent arrival, the duke's sister's son, Lord Thomas.

Absurd for those gentlemen and their friends to be littered about the lawn in winter, despite the unusually warm weather. Ridiculous, too, to be having a weighted disc throwing competition while attired in the latest, highly impractical fashion.

Penelope touched one of the pins in her tightly knotted hair and then rested her hand against the neckline of her outdated muslin. Unexpected discomfort blossomed in her chest. Hot, outsized discomfort.

Had Mr. Anthony, Lord Thomas, and their friends no shame? Even now, beyond the restless channel, young men were sacrificing their lives defending these craggy shores in a war that had already cost Penelope her husband.

"It appears to me"—Penelope's voice tinged with bitterness— "Mr. Anthony and Lord Thomas's only aspiration is a perpetual, decadent house party."

"It is worse than decadence! It is unnatural ambition."

Unnatural ambition? Pen knew them to be irresponsible, certainly, but to accuse them of intentionally usurping the duchy's power?

"Don't you see?" Mrs. Renton asked. "Mr. Anthony brought suit to have your husband declared dead—you need look no further for evidence."

Penelope turned. "Mr. Anthony claimed the suit was necessary in order to free funds for Thaddeus." That was, however, before they'd discovered the surprise codicil to Cheverley's will granting Penelope full possession of Pensteague.

"Mr. Anthony," Mrs. Renton replied, "also claims His Grace is in complete accord with every decision he makes. But, you've seen for yourself—His Grace's words are unintelligible. As for Lord Thomas, he often returns late"—Mrs. Renton lowered her voice—"smelling of tipple and perfume."

Penelope frowned. The amorous exploits of her husband's cousin weren't any of her concern.

On the other hand, she could not deny His Grace's troubling condition. The duke's blank stare had sent shivers through her spine. For the first time, she'd felt a measure of compassion toward the tyrant.

But compassion for the duke and a willingness to intercede on his behalf were two very different positions.

"If those actions weren't awful enough," Mrs. Renton continued, "several women have left our employ so distressed they did not request references. The remaining women serve as mistresses and little else."

Penelope's flush spread to her cheeks. A man had to be vile-hearted to take advantage of anyone in their employ in such a way. "If you would, Mrs. Renton, supply the names and direction of those who left. I will provide references for them from Pensteague."

"Thank you, Lady Cheverley." Mrs. Renton bobbed a short curtsey. "But what of Mr. Anthony and Lord Thomas?"

Penelope gazed back out to the lawn. Were they merely reckless libertines as she'd long assumed, or were they greedy, dangerous men emboldened by the duke's illness, Thaddeus's youth, and his mother's perceived lack of connections?

Anthony had come to Ithwick following the duke's sudden illness and—at Piers's request—had taken over the duties of steward. After Pier's death, Lord Thomas had arrived. They'd been indifferent to Penelope and only cursorily interested in Thaddeus, and she was happy enough to allow things to remain as they were.

But what if they were intentionally robbing Ithwick? What remedy could she bring? She'd need solicitors, barristers, and witnesses to bring suit.

Though Pensteague thrived, she returned every sixpence earned to the estate...the only way she could care for the wounded seamen who regularly appeared on Pensteague's doorstep.

She'd taken the land her husband, Cheverley, had been granted as part of his mother's marriage settlement—a small cottage with surrounding forests and wastes—and transformed it into a thriving estate with choice livestock, crops, fallows, and coppiced wood. She'd raised Thaddeus without assistance from his ducal grandparents. She'd remained dutiful and loyal to Cheverley—and, by extension the duchy—all while striving to provide the wounded seamen Pensteague sheltered the dignity of a generous livelihood. And now, Pensteague was hers and hers alone.

Why should she place all she protected and all she'd built at risk?

"Mrs. Renton," she began, "you've always shown me kindness—"

"You were devoted to young Lord Cheverley," Mrs. Renton interrupted, sniffling. "I had hoped—"

"Allow me to speak plain." Penelope's own dashed hopes were difficult enough to bear, thank you. "To Lord Cheverley's family —everyone but the late duchess—I have always been an inter-loper. It is not my place to interfere."

"But there is no one else," Mrs. Renton replied. "Mr. Anthony acts as if he is master of Ithwick. You are the only one who can stop him."

"Mr. Anthony has been inclined to be pompous for as long as I have known him." But pompous and criminal did not negate one another, did they?

Pen attempted to rationalize again. "Isn't it natural Mr. Anthony take an interest in running the estate? He is, after Thad-deus, the next in line to inherit."

"Mr. Anthony and his coterie are draining the coffers. They are depleting the livestock. Their mismanagement is so severe, long-time tenants are choosing not to renew their leases. Please help us, Lady Cheverley. If you do not protect Ithwick, I fear there will be nothing left for young Thaddeus to inherit." Mrs. Renton paced the length of the rug, paused, then glanced up at a painting. "If Lord Cheverley were here now, it's what he would wish you to do."

Pen's lips flattened at the invocation of her husband's name. Reluctantly, she turned her gaze to the painting she'd avoided since entering the room—a portrait of Cheverley and his older brother as boys.

Though in the portrait, Cheverley's pale blonde hair had yet to darken, his stance already hinted at future swagger. His sheepish half-smile acknowledged worlds he had yet to understand, let alone conquer, but his pale blue eyes alit with a sickle-sharp cunning and an insatiable thirst for adventure.

A thirst that would rob her of a husband and Thaddeus of a father.

Tears pricked the corners of her eyes. Foolish, foolish man.

She did not, however, regret their brief affair and whirlwind marriage. The experience had been transformative and grand—to the extent her sixteen-year-old mind could comprehend grand— a rush that had taken her from the threshold of womanhood to the full blossom of her feminine power. And what followed, though unpleasant, had been the gauntlet that formed her character.

She sighed.

Thirteen years had passed since she'd seen her husband, six since he disappeared off the coast of France, though she hadn't known the gut-wrenching details of his final hours until the recent trial to prove his death.

Cheverley's ship had left the Channel Fleet on orders to capture a French privateer. Soon after the privateer was won, Chev ordered his first mate to sail home the prize. Then, a sudden storm parted the ships, pushing the HMS Defiance off her reckoning by three degrees. But three mere degrees had altered the ship's course enough for the naval gunner to meet a gruesome, rocky end.

In the horrible hours it took the hull to break to pieces, Chev sent part of his crew in a cutter, hopeful they'd find harbor. He remained with his ship...exactly what Penelope would expect of her husband—always certain he could find or forge a way, always driven to display mythic heroism, even at the expense of those he held dear.

In this case, Chev failed. The cutter capsized. The few survivors drifted for days before being rescued. As for Cheverley…after reviewing the evidence, a judge declared him dead. No man, he said, could have survived the wreck.

Then again, her husband had not been just any man.

A burst of low, male laughter rose up from the lawn.

"They laugh while they drain the duchy dry," Mrs. Renton murmured. "They wouldn't have dared to set foot in the house in the first place if…if…"

"…If Lord Cheverley were here," Pen finished quietly.

Yes, she was weary. Yes, she could not spare the expense.

But could she truly turn her back on this part of her husband's past, forever denying skeletons that were not so much in a cupboard as atop a neighboring hill?

"Perhaps," Mrs. Renton whispered, "Lord Cheverley will yet return."

Penelope's neck prickled.

If she were honest, on nights when the moon's glow brightened the sheets of her marriage bed, loneliness pierced her heart like one of her husband's hand-crafted arrows, and she sometimes allowed herself to imagine Cheverley would return.

"Mrs. Renton"—she squelched irrational hope—"we must be careful what we wish. If Cheverley survived, a terrible fate must have befallen him. If he is alive, he is suffering."

She turned away from the portrait.

What would Chev have wanted her to do? If he were here, he would have wanted her to remain tucked up in the proper little jewel casing he'd prepared while he forged forth to set everything to rights in a spectacular show.

But he wasn't here. He hadn't been here for thirteen years.

The better question was—what did she wish to do? How much of what she'd built in Cheverley's name could she risk?

She turned about, taking in the ducal library and considering the stern faces of her husband's ancestors glaring down from centuries past.

If Mr. Anthony and Lord Thomas were corrupt, what would she be teaching Thaddeus if she remained ensconced in comfort while corruption flourished?

Corruption bred fear. Fear bred distrust, anger, divisions and even—if left unchecked—bloodshed.

She did have a responsibility, loath as she was to admit it. Whatever the cost now, it would pale in comparison to the future cost if these men succeeded in fully usurping the duchy's power. She must find a way to root out and remove the corruption. Not only for Thaddeus's sake, but for the sake of those, like Mrs. Renton, whose livelihoods depended on Ithwick.

"Mrs. Renton, I concede." Lord help her. "Thaddeus and I will take up residence at Ithwick, care for the duke and keep a close eye on Mr. Anthony and Lord Thomas. Having the heir and his mother present should gentle the worst of their conduct."

"And if they ask why?"

"I will tell them I intend to weave a shroud for Cheverley on the medieval loom upstairs."

"Bless you, my lady." Mrs. Renton's brows knit. "But is it wise to bring young Thaddeus? As Thaddeus's guardian, Lord Thomas could make trouble."

Let him try.

"Thaddeus goes where I go." In fact, Thaddeus was so protective, she couldn't have confined him to Pensteague if she wished. "Besides, both the duke and Lord Thomas serve as guardians. Thomas cannot assert himself without exposing the duke's state. And, in a few months, Thaddeus will be fourteen—old enough to choose his own guardians."

She recast her gaze toward the group of gentlemen below. Another drunken cheer rose from the lawn.

"You needn't worry any longer, Mrs. Renton." She spoke with

bravado she did not feel. "I will become Ithwick's unlikely champion."

But were her adversaries indolent man-children, or were they a crawling nest of vipers?

And, if they were a nest of vipers—she chilled—which would be the first to sting?

Book Two of the Mythic Duke Trilogy: His Duchess at Eventide

AUTHOR'S NOTE

Lovers of history may recognize the love triangle between Admiral Nelson, Lady Nelson and Lady Hamilton. I included some historical details from that triangle—young Captain Nelson met his wife in the Caribbean, and his mistress when she fell into his arms weeping with gratitude for his service. Also accurate are descriptions of his death, the countess's obsession with his bloody coat, and a disputed codicil that claimed his daughter. That is where the similarities end. The characters in *Her Duke at Daybreak*, their natures, and their motivations are entirely fictional.

Nelson did not impoverish his family. The codicil requested that the Admiralty 'remember' Lady Hamilton. They did not. While they spent extravagant sums on his funeral, Lady Hamilton was left impoverished and in unimaginable debt. She died in exile in France. Only then did Nelson's family take in Nelson's daughter, Horatia. Horatia had once sat on the knee of the Prince Regent, but was treated as little more than a servant by Nelson's heirs. Eventually, she married a country clergyman. She lived out the rest of her life in modest comfort. Lady Nelson never remarried. Lady Nelson and Lady Hamilton remained devoted to Nelson's memory. Neither—to recorded knowledge—took lovers after his death.

For a wealth of information on the ever-fascinating Emma Hamilton and her love affair with Lord Nelson, including pictures of some of their descendants, see the Emma Hamilton Society. I also highly recommend the book *England's Mistress* written by Kate Williams.

And, on a final note, Ashbey's father is modeled after William Byron, 5th Baron Byron, whose story I encountered while researching *Lady Vice*. He was convicted of manslaughter for the murder of his relative, but released after he paid a small fine. He was never tried for the murder of his coachman, whose body he deposited on top of his wife. It is said that his pet crickets left his house en masse the day he died.

ACKNOWLEDGMENTS

In September of 2016, I had the honor of being included as an author in the first Historical Romance Reader's retreat. The conference was magical. I cannot describe what a thrill it was to spend a weekend with other lovers of history and romance.

The impetus for this story came out of a somewhat raucous, thoroughly enjoyable dinner with KJ Jackson, Ava Stone, the fabulous sisters Moll & Em. I'm indebted to the conference organizers, Renee Bernard and Delilah Marvelle, whose combined creativity resulted in an unforgettable event that reignited my passion for writing and for the genre, and to my friend Alice, a dedicated Historical Romance reader, for being a wonderful roommate. I'd like to provide a list of everyone who made that experience so special, but I'll refrain, as it would continue for at least another page.

I'd also like to thank Madeline Iva for keeping me on track, The Killion Group for their graphic design, editorial and formatting resources, Gina Danna for her comments, Mary Behre, Sally MacKenzie and the Washington Romance Writers for an inspiring 2017 Retreat, Stacey Adgern for traveling into the city to write with me, Madeline Martin for a weekend of sprints that shaped the first draft, Talia Surova, and, the writing sisters of my heart, Inara Scott, Susan Sey and Alison Delaine.

Then of course there is my family. The Gavels, my Mom and wonderful sisters, Jo-el and Charlotte, the La Capras, my various nieces and nephews, and the two people I depend on most, Debbie & Richard.

ABOUT WENDY

Historical Romance author Wendy LaCapra writes award-winning books reviewers describe as 'heart-pounding, entrancing', 'lusciously romantic and sparkling with wit.' As a teen, Wendy discovered spine-tingling gothics in her local public library, inspiring her to craft her own seductive tales full of secrets and scandal. She lives with her husband in a quirky, historic building in NYC and loves a girls' night in. For new release, sale alerts and other news, sign up at http://bit.ly/GetWendyNews

BOOKS BY WENDY LACAPRA

Excerpts available for all books on Wendy's Website

The Mythic Duke Series
Her Duke at Daybreak
His Duchess at Eventide
Her Duke at Midnight

The Furies Series
Lady Vice
Lady Scandal
Duchess Decadence

The Lords of Chance
Scandal in Spades
Heart's Desire
Diamond in the Rogue

A Free Lords of Chance-related Novella
Mrs. Sartin's Secretary